Max put his mug down at last. "Dad's left some money to Annie."

Samantha gasped at the figure he named. "I never imagined… How very generous of him."

"Dad was crazy about Annie," Max said dryly. "His only grandchild. He would have done anything for her."

"He did love her, I know." Samantha felt a lump in her throat as she remembered the bond between Annie and her grandfather.

Max was watching her closely, and she knew he had noticed her emotion. "The point is," he said, "the inheritance comes with a condition."

"A condition?" She was wary now.

"For Annie to get her inheritance, the two of you have to come back home."

In an instant, Samantha was rigid with shock. "I don't believe it! Your father knew why I left. I can't believe he'd have done this to me!"

"It's hardly a life sentence," Max said sarcastically. "It's not as if you have to stay forever. Six months, that's all."

"Six months! Six weeks would be too much. Six days. Even one day."

Rosemary Carter was born in South Africa, but has lived in Canada for many years with her husband and three children. Although her home is on the prairies, not far from the beautiful Rockies, she still retains her love of the South African bushveld, which is why she sometimes likes to set her stories there. Both Rosemary and her husband enjoy concerts, theater, opera and hiking in the mountains. Reading was always her passion, and led to her first attempts at writing stories herself.

A Wife Worth
Keeping
Rosemary Carter

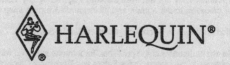

TORONTO • NEW YORK • LONDON
AMSTERDAM • PARIS • SYDNEY • HAMBURG
STOCKHOLM • ATHENS • TOKYO • MILAN • MADRID
PRAGUE • WARSAW • BUDAPEST • AUCKLAND

ISBN 0-373-03602-7

A WIFE WORTH KEEPING

First North American Publication 2000.

Copyright © 2000 by Rosemary Carter.

CHAPTER ONE

"Max!"

Samantha stared in astonishment at the tall, dark-haired man by the window. The last thing she had expected when she walked into her apartment was to see her husband— her very soon to be *ex*-husband, she corrected herself.

"What the heck is he doing here?" Brian muttered resentfully, coming up behind her.

Before anyone could answer him, a tiny human cannon-ball hurled itself past the two adults and into the arms of the dark-haired man. *"Daddy!"* four-year-old Annie shouted excitedly.

Holding her to him, Max kissed the top of the wind-blown head. "How's my girl?"

"Great! Mommy didn't say you were coming."

Deliberately, giving herself time to control the excitement that took hold of her whenever she saw Max—an emotion that was totally unjustified in light of the fact that she had left him because of his blatant infidelity—Samantha put down the picnic basket.

"I didn't know he was coming, honey," she told the child.

"Been on an outing?" Max asked.

Samantha shrugged. "As you see." At the same moment, Annie gave her own animated explanation: "We went to the park, Daddy."

The tall man hugged her again. "Have fun, princess?"

"Oh yes! I fed the ducks."

Samantha took the father-daughter moment to study Max. The last time she had seen him had been at the funeral

5

of his father, just over a month ago. Although he came regularly to visit with Annie, he hadn't been here since then; probably because he had been tied up with his father's affairs.

He was looking tired, Samantha thought, and a little drawn. She knew how close he had been to his father, and how saddened he was by his death. She, too, had felt the loss keenly, for William Anderson had taken on the role of a father after her marriage to Max—her own parents had died in a motor accident years earlier—and her affection for the kind and distinguished elderly gentleman hadn't faded when life with his son had become intolerable.

Warily she eyed that son now. Despite his fatigue, he was still dynamic. But it was not only his striking good looks that had made her fall head over heels in love with Max five years earlier. His quick intelligence had appealed to her own curious mind, his dry humor had made her laugh. As for his sexiness—a vibrant sexiness that even fatigue could not diminish—that had struck an instant cord deep inside her. The cord still existed, even after everything that had happened. She wished it did not, but so far she had been helpless to do anything about it.

Brian, three years younger than Max, blond, blue-eyed, a little pink after a day in the sun, couldn't begin to compare with him. No man could, Samantha acknowledged grimly. The fact was no cause for joy.

"Did I make a mistake with the day?" she asked, puzzled. In the time since they had been apart, Max had had regular visits with Annie: angry though Samantha was with him, she knew how important it was for their child to maintain contact with her father. "Did I forget a visit with Annie?"

Max shook his head.

"Then why are you here?"

"We need to talk."

"Talk?" Samantha was suddenly furious. "You could have told me you were coming."

"I didn't know till this morning I'd be able to make it. And when I called, there was no answer." A cool glance at Brian. "You must have been gone by then."

"You could have tried another day in that case. I guess that didn't occur to you?"

"You guess right."

"Why didn't you try again, Max?" Samantha demanded. Beside her, she sensed that Brian was bristling with resentment.

"Didn't think it was necessary."

Max didn't look in the least apologetic, standing there with his head slightly tilted in the autocratic manner she remembered so well. He was putting her in the wrong, Samantha knew, and she understood that she had to stand up to him.

Bending down to Annie, she said, "Sweetheart, why don't you go and wash your hands after feeding the ducks?" And when the excited little girl had rushed off, she straightened up and turned on Max.

"You're making a statement, aren't you?" The words were an accusation rather than a question. "Forcing your way into my apartment without so much as a by your leave."

"I do have a key," he reminded her.

"Only because you were once welcome to use it."

Max grinned at her, a wicked grin that sent a quick shiver through Samantha. She had been living in the apartment, a legacy from her parents, at the time that she had met Max. Sentiment had caused her to keep it even after their marriage, a decision for which she was very grateful now, for it required most of her secretarial salary to maintain Annie and herself without accepting any of the financial help Max had offered.

There had been many an ecstatic night spent in these rooms, hours when she and Max had abandoned themselves to the love that had developed like wildfire between them. A virgin until she met him, Samantha had never imagined she had it in her to be quite so passionate. They had had some memorable times in the apartment. Her cheeks flushed at one particular memory. That wicked grin of Max's told her that he hadn't forgotten, either.

"I should have taken the key from you months ago," she said hotly.

His eyes glinted. "Don't you think you're overreacting?"

"Dammit, man!" Brian cut in angrily. "How dare you talk to Samantha like this? This is her apartment, and you have absolutely no right to be here without her permission."

Max turned to Samantha. "Who is this man?"

"Brian Landers. A friend of mine."

Max held out his hand to Brian. "Max Anderson, since my wife hasn't seen fit to introduce us properly."

Declining the proffered hand, Brian took a step backward. Max, Samantha noted, was not in the least discomforted—if anything, he looked amused.

"She's not your wife." Brian's eyes were stormy.

"Actually she is—or didn't she tell you?"

"Legally. Not in any other way. And not for long, either."

"You seem to know a lot about us," Max drawled.

Tensely Samantha watched the two men. She could almost touch the animosity that crackled between them. Max was baiting Brian deliberately, and Brian, sweet Brian, was letting him do it.

"You'll be divorced soon. And when it's all over, Samantha and I are going to be married."

Samantha darted a startled glance at Brian, who looked back at her defiantly. He knew as well as she did that casual friendship was all she was interested in. It was true he had spoken of marriage, but she had told him more than once that it was not in the cards as far as she was concerned. Though not content with the situation, he had seemed to accept it. Why complicate matters now? Samantha knew the answer, of course: Brian was baiting Max, too. But this wasn't the time to take him up on it. Besides, it might not be a bad idea if Max thought she had plans for the future.

"Congratulations." Max's expression was difficult to read. "The fact is, at this moment Samantha is still my wife, and we have things to talk about." He paused. "In private," he added pointedly.

"You have some nerve!" Brian exclaimed, his cheeks reddening. "And if you think—"

"I think you should go now," Samantha intervened, as gently as she could.

"I have no intention of leaving you with this brute!"

"Max won't hurt me, and he's right, it's best if we talk alone."

Brian's face tightened in an expression Samantha had never seen before. His hands clenched, and for a moment she wondered whether he was going to be stubborn and refuse to go. Max waited calmly. He looked strong and sure of himself in a way that Brian could never be.

A moment passed, then Brian seemed to realize he had met his match. "Okay, I'll leave. Call you later."

His eyes never leaving Max's face, he bent and kissed Samantha hard on the mouth—the kind of kiss he hadn't attempted before. He left the apartment then, slamming the door behind him.

When Brian was gone, Max gave Annie a new doll. The

little girl was ecstatic. No matter how many dolls she owned, each new one was welcomed with the same degree of delight. At her father's suggestion, she took it to her room, so that she could introduce it to the rest of her doll family.

"You left me for a man like that?" Max said, when Annie was safely out of earshot. His voice was heavy with sarcasm.

Samantha stared at him angrily. "You know why I left you. Why exactly are you here, Max?"

"Is it true you're going to marry him?"

She would never marry Brian: after seeing him with Max, she was certain of it. However difficult her life was, she couldn't marry a man she didn't love and respect. But Max did not have to know that; in fact, it was important that he didn't.

"My future is none of your concern, Max."

"Wrong, Samantha." His face was hard, his voice dangerous. "Whatever concerns Annie concerns me, too. Brian, or any other man you may link up with, is very much my concern, and you'd better remember that."

Tensely Samantha looked at Max, so handsome, and at the same time so arrogant. "You never said why you're here."

Max pushed his hair from his forehead in a gesture that Samantha recognized of old. He looked, very suddenly, almost vulnerable, and Samantha was swept with unexpected emotion. In that moment she wanted nothing more than to put her arms around him, to hold him close and kiss away his sadness.

Involuntarily she took a step toward him. And then she remembered what Max had done to her—*she could not let herself forget*—and she moved away from him.

"You said you wanted to talk, Max."

"Yes."

"Well then, shoot, and after that you can go."

Annie ran into the room at that moment. "Will you play with me, Daddy?"

Max darted Samantha a quick look. "Sure I will, princess," he said then to Annie. "What shall we play?"

She held out the new doll to him. "Baby needs to go to bed."

"I'll make you some supper while Daddy plays with you. And then it's time for your bedtime, too, honey," said Samantha. And in an undertone to Max, "We'll talk after that."

She went to the kitchen, and began to scramble an egg for Annie. When she returned to the living room, father and daughter were engrossed in a private world of their own. Sitting on the carpet with Annie, Max had lost the autocratic expression he sometimes wore: with his child he was all gentleness and fun. No wonder, Samantha thought, that Annie looked forward so much to his visits. Max was a good father. If only he had been as good a husband.

After Annie had eaten her supper and had been tucked up in bed, Max finally announced his reason for arriving without warning.

"You and Annie have to come back home."

Samantha stared at Max disbelievingly. "I can't believe you wasted your time coming here to tell me that. We'll be divorced soon."

"The divorce is your choice, Samantha. You know I've never wanted it. I always wanted our family to stay together."

Samantha did not answer immediately. If she was honest with herself, she knew she didn't want the divorce, either. Emotions swirled within her as she looked at Max—as much as she tried to tell herself otherwise, she understood that she still loved him. Perhaps she would never really be free of him. But that didn't alter the fact that what he had done was unforgivable, and that she would always despise herself if she agreed to go back to him.

"Damn you, Max, you had a fine way of showing your attachment to your family," she said at last, fiercely.

"Samantha—"

"There isn't a day when I don't think of you and Edna in bed together. I feel sick whenever I remember."

"You never let me talk about it."

"And I won't talk now! So if that's all you came about, you really did waste your time. And mine," she added. "Brian was right, you do have a nerve barging in here without invitation or permission. If it means anything, I was looking forward to spending the evening with Brian. As soon as you go, I'll call him and see if he'd like to come back."

Pointedly she looked at the door. But Max did not take the hint.

"You don't want to hear about Edna? Fine," he said, "but you'll listen to what I came here to say."

She shook her head, "Whatever it is, I really don't think I'd be interested."

"You can't know—without hearing it. I absolutely insist you give me a few minutes of your time."

Recognizing the authority in his tone, Samantha knew he wouldn't go till she'd heard him out. "Seems I have no choice," she said reluctantly.

He threw her a half grin. "I'm parched. How about making us some coffee?"

Max still had all the audacity she remembered so well; for some reason it had always been a part of his appeal. Despite herself, Samantha found herself grinning back at him. "Pushing your luck, aren't you? The coffee in the percolator's still hot, and you know where to find a mug.

Just don't ask me to cook you supper, because I draw the line at that.''

As she watched Max disappear into the kitchen, other memories returned. There had been so many lovely evenings when Max had insisted on making coffee after dinner. "I enjoy spoiling you,'' he'd tell her, handing her an Irish coffee or a cappuccino.

He would sit down close beside her, and she would nestle against him as they sipped their coffee and talked about their day. Samantha would think of how they'd be making love soon, and she would feel a stirring deep inside of her. No matter how often they made love, their delight in each other never grew less. Or so she had believed.

"You look a bit grim,'' Max said, as he came out of the kitchen, carrying two steaming mugs.

"Just waiting for you to get to the point,'' she snapped.

He gave her a mug, and sat down opposite her. Tensely she watched as he took a sip. She could not have said why she dreaded what he was about to say. He was taking his own sweet time about it, too.

After what seemed like an awfully long time, he put down his mug at last. "Dad's will.''

"What about it?''

"He's left some money to Annie. Quite a substantial amount.''

Samantha gasped at the figure he named. "I never imagined... How very generous of him.''

"Dad was crazy about Annie,'' Max said dryly. "His only grandchild. He would have done anything for her.''

"He did love her, I know.'' Samantha felt a lump form in her throat as she remembered the bond between Annie and her grandfather. It had been touching to watch them together, the elderly man and the small girl, linked in a special harmony.

Max was watching her closely, and she knew he had noticed her emotion. "The point is," he said, "the inheritance comes with a condition."

"A condition?" She was wary now.

"For Annie to get her inheritance, the two of you have to come back home."

In an instant, Samantha was rigid with shock. "*I don't believe it!* Didn't William know why I left? I can't believe he'd have done this to me!"

"It's hardly a life sentence," Max said sarcastically. "It's not as if you have to stay forever. Six months, that's all."

"Six months! Six weeks would be too much. Six days. Even one day."

"So melodramatic, Samantha," he taunted.

"I have a life," she said wildly. "A home, a job. Friends. Activities."

Max looked around him with a pointedness that was not lost on her. "Nothing like the home you had. And if I'm to judge by Brian, your friends aren't all that great, either."

Samantha lifted her head. "Don't you dare judge me, Max. Maybe I'm not living the life I used to, but at least I'm in a place of my own, mixing with people I trust."

A shadow seemed to pass before Max's eyes, but he said quietly, "You haven't given me an answer."

"I thought I had," she said restlessly. "It's obvious I can't go back."

"You'd do Annie out of her inheritance?" Max's gaze was on her face.

Standing up abruptly, Samantha went to the window. For a long minute she looked outside, her eyes moving over the vista of skyscrapers and busy traffic, so different from the lush gardens of Max's Long Island home. "It's not fair to put it that way," she said at last.

"I'm just saying it the way it is."

"No, Max." She took a quick step away from the window. "You know as well as I do that you're putting me in an impossible position. Besides, I don't understand. I know William was crazy about Annie. So why—in heaven's name why?—did he make this impossible condition?"

Dark eyes gleamed in the lean, handsome face. "You're intelligent, Samantha—I'm sure you know the answer."

"Emotional blackmail," she told him flatly. "I loved William, and I never imagined he would resort to this kind of tactic."

Once more the dark eyes moved over her face. "Why is it so hard to understand? You knew Dad was upset when you left. He hated seeing our marriage break up."

"Is this his way of trying to patch things up again?"

It was a moment before Max said, "What if it is?"

It was hard to meet the steady eyes. Samantha had to shift her own gaze while she struggled with difficult emotions. At length, she looked back at him. "It can't work, Max. There's no way it could work."

"Sure of that?"

"*Yes!* You betrayed me, Max. I'll never forget it, never forgive. How do you think I could possibly live with you again? I can't look at you for a moment without remembering you and Edna."

"And because of that you'd deprive Annie of her inheritance? Six months, Samantha. That's all Dad asked. Can't you put your grievances behind you for the sake of our child?"

Her hand jerked violently, hitting her coffee mug in the process, so that it almost fell off the table. "Don't try putting a guilt trip on me, Max! Of course I'd like Annie to have her inheritance, but I can't accept the condition. It would never work. I can't come back to you, and that's all there is to it." She made a small gesture. "Please go, Max."

She looked at him, dreading a refusal, but to her relief he stood up.

As the door closed behind him, Samantha's composure crumbled, and she began to tremble. The apartment, the one place in the world that was her haven, was all at once empty. Max's presence had filled the room with an energy that was now gone. Feeling cold suddenly, Samantha went to the kitchen and poured herself more coffee.

She was about to take a sip, when the phone rang. It was Brian, demanding to know whether Max had gone, and wanting to come over. She told him she wasn't feeling up to it, which was true, though not in the way Brian took it. As she replaced the receiver, she knew there was only one person in the world that she really wanted to be with. And she had given up her chance to be with him—probably forever.

Standing beside Annie's bed, Samantha looked down at the child she loved more than life itself—apart from Max, whom she had once loved just as much. Outside, a wind had risen and the first hard drops of rain were beginning to hit the window. Annie's blanket had slipped to her feet, revealing an arm around the new doll. Gently Samantha drew the blanket over the small body, then bent, moved a strand of fair hair from her forehead and kissed a soft cheek.

Annie stirred. "Mommy," she murmured.

"Yes, honey?"

"Is Daddy here?"

"He had to leave. But he'll come and visit again soon."

Annie's eyes opened slightly. 'I wish he lived with us. Can't he, Mommy?"

Samantha's heart gave a little lurch, as it did every time Annie asked the question. "No, Annie, Daddy has his home and we have ours. But you know he loves you very much, and that he's with you whenever he can be.''

The answer seemed to satisfy the little girl, for her eyelids drooped, and within seconds her breathing was as slow and peaceful as before. Her mother, on the other hand, felt anything but peaceful.

Seeing Max always unsettled her. Each time, she wondered how his relationship with Edna was progressing. Were they officially a couple now? Would he and Edna be married when his divorce from Samantha was final? A part of her longed to know the answers. But she was too proud to ask the questions. She would find out whatever she had to in due time. And she knew already that she would hate the answers.

Edna... Even now, almost a year later, Samantha still felt ill whenever she thought of that terrible night. Max had been attending an office conference out of town, and Samantha had decided to surprise him. She had packed a sexy negligee, left Annie in the loving and capable hands of the housekeeper and her grandfather and driven upstate to the resort where the conference was being held. It was late in the evening by the time she got there, and without stopping to have Max paged—she knew his room number from his phone calls—she made her way straight there. The door was not locked, and still bent on surprising him, she walked right in without knocking.

A surprise it had been—for everyone concerned. Two people were in the bed where there should have been only one. Max, a visibly startled Max, jerked upright, clutching the sheet to his chin. The woman clinging to him laughed, a high, obscene laugh; Samantha could still hear the laughter ringing in her ears at night when she was alone. She recognized her immediately. Edna Blair. Edna was also a lawyer, and Samantha had met her at various social events held by the law firm where Max was a partner.

Edna was naked. Unlike Max, she made no attempt at modesty, but left her part of the sheet draped around her waist. Glossy black hair that was usually swept backward in an elegant chignon now tumbled loosely around her shoulders.

"*Samantha!*" Max's voice was hoarse. "What are you doing here?"

She couldn't answer him. Her legs were so weak that she had to clutch the door handle to stop herself from falling. Nausea, hot and bitter, rose in her throat.

Still without speaking, she stumbled backward through the open doorway. Dimly she heard Max calling out to her, but she didn't stop to listen to what he was saying. Ignoring the curious looks of people in the lobby, she rushed to her car and drove without stopping back to New York. It was well after midnight when she reached Long Island.

The phone rang several times, but she ignored it. She hardly slept that night. By the time Max arrived home early the next morning, she had already packed suitcases for Annie and herself.

"We have to talk," he insisted. "I can explain—"

She turned on him bitterly. "I was in your room. I don't need an explanation!"

"You don't understand, Samantha. Edna and I were just—"

"Having fun when I so inconveniently barged in," she interrupted.

Max's color was high, his eyes stormy. "Sarcasm doesn't suit you, Samantha."

"That's priceless! Really priceless! You are unfaithful, and then you have the nerve to criticize the way I speak. You're even more of a louse than I imagined. Want to know why I came, Max? I had some crazy notion of a romantic weekend. Isn't that wild?''

"My God, Samantha!" His voice sounded raw.

What an actor the man was! No wonder he was so brilliant in court, and that juries were swayed by him. He sounded so utterly genuine, even in the ears of the wife who knew him so well. But he wouldn't succeed in swaying her, he wouldn't sway her ever again.

"Pretty crazy, right, Max?" She closed a suitcase with a bang. "Well, I'm out of here now. I'm leaving."

"You can't mean that." Max looked stricken.

Samantha only looked at him contemptuously.

"And you're taking Annie?" He seemed shattered. He really was an amazing actor. "Samantha—please, just let me speak."

Just for a moment, Samantha was actually tempted to hear what he had to say. Then she gave herself a quick mental shake. She couldn't allow an explanation, no matter how brilliantly he gave it, to stop her from doing what she had to.

"I don't want to hear it, whatever it is." She flashed him a bitter look. "And yes, I'm taking Annie. You'll have visitation rights, of course. However much I detest you—and believe me I do!—I know that Annie needs her father."

He tried to stop her. "You can't just go! Not without hearing me out. Edna and I—it wasn't what you thought."

"Isn't that what people always say when they're caught in the act?"

"There was no act. Nothing happened."

"Give me a break, Max!"

"Just let me tell you about it."

"No!" Samantha clapped her hands over her ears. "Don't you understand, Max? I refuse to hear about Edna. I already know everything I have to. Listening to you trying

to wriggle your way out of it would make me feel even sicker than I do already.''

"This is so frustrating!" Max exclaimed.

"Tough." Samantha picked up a suitcase in each hand. "When I've put all our stuff in the car, we'll be off. You'll be hearing from a lawyer, Max."

Now, as she stood by Annie's bed, with the rain spattering against the window, Samantha tried to push the memories from her mind. She thought of her lovely little girl instead. In the glow of a small bedside light—Annie was nervous of the dark—long lashes cast faint shadows over downy cheeks.

There was something vulnerable and defenseless about the sleeping child. Annie was unable to make decisions concerning her future, no four-year-old could. Looking down at her, Samantha was racked with uncertainty. If only Max had never come to her with his father's idea. She knew that for the rest of her life she would wonder whether she had done the right thing in rejecting it.

"You're thinking of going back to Max?"

Samantha sister, Dorothy, lived in California, and the two of them burned up the telephone wires between the East and West Coasts at least twice a week. Dorothy was Samantha's best friend and confidante, the one person in the world to whom she could bare her heart easily and without regret afterward. Happily married to Arthur, a sweet and gentle soul who would never dream of cheating on his wife, she had been outraged at Max's betrayal.

"It's only just a thought at this point," Samantha said.

"After what the rat did to you?" Dorothy's shudder was almost visible through the telephone line.

"It's not as if I want to go... I don't."

There was a silence, and then Dorothy said, "You're thinking of Annie."

"I have to."

"Well yes, you're her mother. But, Sam, you have a life of your own, too, and you're just beginning to get things together again. You're doing so well—the way you're coping on your own, your job, even a new man in your life— or he would be if you let him."

"Brian will never be more than a friend," Samantha said firmly.

"You're comparing him with Max. Don't do it, Sam— you'll only set yourself up for grief if you do. And for heaven's sake, don't go throwing over everything you've achieved just because Max says the word."

Samantha pushed agitatedly at her blond hair. On the other side of the room, Annie was playing with her puppets: a clown was perched on one hand, a rabbit on the other, and Annie was carrying on an animated conversation between them. Absorbed in a world of her own, the little girl didn't hear her mother's conversation with her aunt. Not that she would have understood its significance if she had.

"That's the thing, I do have to think about Annie," Samantha said at last. "Imagine what I'd be depriving her of if I don't go back to Max. Oh, sure, Dorothy, I'm doing whatever I can for her, but we both know I can never give her anything near as much as her grandfather wanted her to have."

"If he wanted it so badly, he shouldn't have attached any strings."

Dorothy sounded so fierce that Samantha smiled to herself. She could imagine her sister striding around her kitchen, her portable phone clutched tightly to her ear. Dorothy always strode when she felt passionately about something, and she was passionate now.

"According to Max, William was devastated when I left with Annie, and this is his way of trying to fix things."

"Are you saying he condoned his precious son's behavior?"

"I have no idea how much he knew. I certainly didn't tell him, and I don't know how much Max said to him, either. You have to remember that William was already quite ill by the time I left."

"Not so ill that he didn't know how to scheme and manipulate."

"Maybe so, but apparently he wanted very badly to see us together again, and the will was his way of making it happen."

Again there was silence. Yesterday's rain had given the streets a newly washed appearance, and Samantha thought that she would take Annie to the park after the phone call.

"Why do I get the feeling," her sister asked at last, "that you've already made up your mind?"

"Because you understand me well enough to know that I was up half the night agonizing. I'm watching Annie as we talk, sis, and I know I can't deprive her of her inheritance. Just think, Dorothy, there's so much she could do with it one day. She may want to travel the world, or decide on a really special education. There's no limit to the things Annie may want to do. How can I rob her of her chances?" Samantha paused. "She might never forgive me."

"Then you're going back to Max." It wasn't a question.

"I think I have to," Samantha said slowly. "It's only for six months. Somehow I'll get through it."

"But what about Annie getting upset when she had to leave her daddy again?"

"I'll do my best to make sure she's not hurt. But she's only four, and children are very adaptable at that age."

"And where does his lordship fit into all this?"

"Platonically." Samantha's voice had a hard edge. "Despite William's motives, Max will have to understand that.

Remembering Edna, I shouldn't think he would want it any other way, either.''

"You still have feelings for him, don't you?" Dorothy asked softly.

Samantha swallowed on a hard lump in her throat. "Yes—God help me, and you're the only person in the world I'd admit it to. But whatever my feelings, I'll never allow Max Anderson to hurt me again, and that means keeping my distance from him. Six months, Dorothy, and I'll be back here in Manhattan. It's the way it's going to be.''

CHAPTER TWO

IF MAX was surprised when Samantha called the next morning, his tone didn't show it. "Dad would've been glad," was all he said.

"Are you?" The question was out before Samantha could stop it.

Max only laughed softly.

Riled, she persisted. "Well, are you?"

"I believe you're doing the right thing for Annie, and obviously I'm glad about that."

Fool, she thought bitterly, what other answer had she expected? Whatever her own feelings might be for Max, his affair with Edna had made it abundantly clear that he no longer loved Samantha.

"One condition," she said, as briskly as she could. "Don't flaunt that woman in front of me while I'm at the house. The next time I catch the two of you in bed, I'll be out of your house, no questions asked. If Annie loses her inheritance as a result, you'll do your own explaining to her one day."

"Samantha, about Edna—"

"When will you understand that I refuse to hear about her?" Samantha said vehemently. Her tone became more matter-of-fact as she continued. "I'll need to arrange a six-month absence from work—heaven only knows if they'll give it to me, I may have to leave if they don't."

"You won't know till you talk to them." Max paused. "One other thing, Samantha."

"Yes?"

"The divorce proceedings will have to be put on hold for six months."

"*Why?*" Samantha gripped the receiver tightly.

"Think about it. We can't be attempting a reconciliation at the same time as we're getting divorced."

"Even though the reconciliation is just a sham?" she asked bitterly.

"Even though. If word were to get out that we aren't really trying, Annie would lose her inheritance."

After a moment, Samantha asked, "Why do I feel as if I'm in some kind of trap?"

"I have no idea."

"Sure you do! The divorce gets back on track the day the six months are up, Max."

"I didn't say it wouldn't," he responded, so pleasantly that Samantha could have throttled him.

She was about to put down the phone, when Max said, "Samantha—will you try to enjoy the six months?"

Her entire body tightened at the question. She had tried telling herself that her only reason for agreeing to the outrageous proposal was to safeguard Annie's inheritance. And still she was aware that a part of her—an annoyingly treacherous part— wanted nothing more than to go back to the house where she had once been so blissfully happy. She would have to watch herself: Max must never know that her feelings for him were as intense as ever.

Gripping the telephone receiver tightly, she said, "*Enjoy?* You must be kidding, Max! I'm only coming back for one reason, and as far as I'm concerned the time won't pass quickly enough."

Brian was incredulous when she told him her decision. His face whitened with anger. He couldn't believe she would even consider going back to the man who had betrayed her. He tried everything in his power to dissuade her, and refused to accept her explanation.

"Does this mean you're giving up on your divorce? Because if you are, I can tell you you're in for trouble. Max Anderson is a jerk. I know his type, I could tell the moment I laid eyes on him."

His tone was more belligerent than Samantha had ever heard it. Instinctively words leaped to her tongue in defense of Max, but she managed to suppress them before they made it past her lips. Max *was* a jerk—in capitals—Brian was right about that, and it made no sense at all that she didn't want to hear someone else say it. As calmly as she could, she made it clear that she had not changed her mind about the divorce. She decided not to mention the fact that the proceedings were going into temporary limbo: for one thing, she could not face more tension; for another the matter was none of Brian's concern.

"We'll be married the moment it comes through," he insisted.

"No." She spoke quietly. "I told you from the start we could only be friends. That hasn't changed, Brian. Your friendship means a lot to me, and you're wonderful with Annie, but I'm determined to give myself lots of time before rushing into another permanent relationship."

"I'll wait for you," he vowed.

Samantha wished she didn't find his intensity so offputting. Even more, she wished she didn't find Brian so totally lacking beside Max. She would have to learn not to compare every man she met with her soon to be ex-husband, for if she did, she would never have a future.

"Don't wait for me, there's no point in it," she said firmly. " In fact, I really wish you would start seeing other women."

*   *   *

"Home," Max said, as he turned the car through the gates and onto the long sweeping driveway.

"Yes." Samantha's voice was not quite steady.

Tears came to her eyes at sight of the beautiful house. The red-gold brick walls glowed in the late-afternoon sunset, and the garden was as beautiful as ever. The roses were in bloom, and the lawn was thick and lush as a carpet. She turned her head quickly away from Max and toward Annie in the back seat, glad that the little girl's excitement gave her a brief opportunity to escape Max's scrutiny.

"We're home?" Annie shouted gleefully.

The house on Long Island was just far enough from Manhattan that Max had not taken the child there in the course of their outings: instead, they had gone to places closer to Samantha's apartment. Even her visits with her beloved grandfather had taken place in the city when he'd been well enough to accompany Max. Annie had not been back to her old home since leaving it with her mother.

"Yes, princess," Max answered before Samantha could speak, his own voice a little husky. "Look, Annie, your swings and your sandbox."

"My very own park!" Annie exclaimed. "That's so neat!"

The two adults shared a smile—their first moment of mutual amusement since their parting, Samantha realized.

The gardener said hello to her as Max parked the car, and inside the house, Helen, the housekeeper, was waiting to greet them. Hugging Annie, she took her off to the kitchen where some special treats awaited her.

"Welcome home," Max said softly, as they went further.

"Don't use that word." Samantha's tone was short.

"You didn't seem to mind the first time, in the car."

"You caught me off guard. But this isn't my home, Max, and in the circumstances the word isn't appropriate."

"No harm in being friendly." His eyes were thoughtful. "Make things a lot easier in the long run."

"As long as the friendliness isn't phony—I couldn't live with that."

And then they were walking through the house, with its large, elegantly furnished rooms. At the bottom of the spiral staircase leading up to the bedrooms, Samantha paused. Involuntarily she glanced at Max. His eyes met hers and, as if he knew exactly what she was thinking—which he probably did—one winged eyebrow lifted, giving him an enigmatic expression.

Resolutely Samantha marched past him and began to walk up the stairs. Carrying a suitcase in each hand, Max followed behind her. There were five bedrooms, and outside the door of the first one, Samantha hesitated. This had been her father-in-law's room, William's haven, where he had spent more and more of his time in the last few years of his life.

"I can't believe he isn't here anymore," she said unsteadily. Briefly she turned to Max. "He was such an integral part of this house."

"That's right, he was."

She heard the grief in Max's voice, and had to fight the urge to reach out to him. And then she reminded herself that he had managed very well without her until now, and would do so again. Edna, Samantha told herself cynically, was the person he would turn to if he needed emotional support.

Annie's room was next. The door was open, and Samantha saw that the room had been redecorated. The walls had a fresh coat of pale pink paint, and there was a new comforter on the bed. Lying against the pillow was yet another new doll with curly blond hair and a frilly dress. In a strange way, the doll looked a little like Annie.

Samantha felt a small shiver of fear as she looked around her. "So many changes," she said, turning to Max.

"I want Annie to be happy here." He was smiling, but Samantha felt suddenly as if the walls were closing in on her.

She met his gaze. "Annie's home is with me, Max."

"Of course."

In the car, and then again outside William's room, there had been fleeting moments of rapport. Now, Samantha felt an uneasiness, which she made every effort to hide.

Fiercely she said, "Just as long as you understand that. You can see Annie as often as you like—I will never try to keep her from you—but when I go, she goes with me. So don't start having any fancy ideas, Max. We're here for six months, and the day the time is up we'll be out of here."

His gaze lingered on turbulent green eyes. "You make it sound as if you're in some kind of prison."

She made herself hold that gaze. "A prison with shining gold bars and all the luxuries the prisoners could possibly want. You've thought it all out, haven't you, Max? But I warn you, don't make it too tempting. I don't want Annie yearning for this place when it's time to leave."

"You're sure you'll want to go?"

The question was so unexpected that for a moment Samantha couldn't answer. Then she said, "*Yes!* I can't stand the thought of being here! And if it weren't for your father's will, you wouldn't want me here, either. Be honest, Max, admit you want the time to pass as quickly as I do."

His eyes glittered. "Don't ever make the mistake of thinking you can read my mind, Samantha. You can't."

She looked at him quickly, sensing there was more to his words than he was saying. When he didn't elaborate, she said, "I used to think I understood you. Obviously I was wrong."

"Completely wrong," said her soon-to-be ex-husband.

And then they were walking further. To say that Samantha was astonished when they went right past the guest room would have been an understatement. Her heart began a furious beating as she saw Max go into the master bedroom. She hesitated a moment, then followed him in. He was already putting down the cases when she turned to him.

"I'm not going to be sleeping here—surely?"

"Where else?" Max's eyes glittered with amusement.

"The guest room, of course," she said quickly.

"This was always your room," he reminded her. "*Our* room."

She couldn't stop the flush that spread quickly to her cheeks. But she managed to say hardily, "When we were married."

"We still are."

Samantha wondered how he could be so calm. "Technically—because the divorce hasn't come through yet."

"Dad wanted us to try again. You knew that when you agreed to come back."

Samantha looked around her, knowing she shouldn't be surprised at the welter of emotions that made her feel weak. *Until death do us part.* The words had meant so much to her at the wedding ceremony five years earlier. Looking up at Max through a shimmer of happy tears, she had been so certain they would be together all their lives. She had entered marriage with a sense of absolute commitment, and it had never occurred to her that Max had not felt the same way. How wrong she had been!

The lovely room, with its thick cream carpet and the spectacular view across the garden to the blue water of the Sound, had once borne the stamp of Samantha's taste and femininity. That had changed, too. She couldn't have said exactly what it was, but something masculine had invaded the room. Perhaps it was the absence of the flowers that had always adorned the table by the window, or the personal photos missing from the dresser, but somehow the room was not quite as she remembered it.

Her voice shook as she said, "Annie is my reason for coming here. My *only* reason, Max. You have to be clear about that."

"I thought you were attached to Dad," he said quietly.

"I *loved* your father. Never doubt that for a moment. But I hate the fact that he decided to meddle in our lives. Surely you feel the same way?"

"His motives were good," Max said, without answering the question.

"I know that, and I understand what he was trying to do, but as far as our marriage is concerned—it's dead, Max. Incapable of being resuscitated. You and I both know that. I just wish William had accepted it."

The look he subjected her to was searching. "Can you tell me, honestly, that coming back home means nothing to you?"

"I asked you not to call it home," Samantha said vehemently. "Can't you understand that it's not our home any longer? Mine and Annie's? It's just a house—a very beautiful house—but that's all it is for us now."

Max shrugged. "If you say so."

She took a breath. "And in case... In case you have any thoughts of sharing this room with me—it's not on, Max."

"Just where do you propose I sleep?" His tone was sardonic.

"In the guest room. Unless you'd prefer me to sleep there? It's where I thought I'd be all along."

Unexpectedly Max grinned—a sparkling-eyed grin that sent the blood racing through her veins. "Oh, no, my darling wife. You'll sleep right here. If it's what you want, I'll move to the guest room—for the moment."

"For the moment?" she made herself ask.

"Until you invite me back in here."

"Hell will freeze over before that happens!" she exclaimed, though more unsteadily than she would have wished: Max's endearment—facetious though it was—had knocked her for more of a loop than she cared to admit to herself.

"Long before that, I think," he said, still with that disturbing grin.

"Think away. Incidentally, skip the 'darling' stuff, Max. It makes me sick to hear it."

"Some habits die hard, Samantha—it's what I always called you."

"Long ago."

"Not all that long."

His eyes lingered on her lips in a way she had once found indescribably seductive. Still did, unfortunately. She suppressed a small shiver.

"Long enough! At this point, I can't even bear to be in the same room as you."

Max laughed, the sound as low and vital as she remembered. "Liar," he drawled. "Whatever else may have happened in the past, at least one thing hasn't changed."

"I don't want to hear this! Any of it." In an instant, she was as tight as a coiled spring. "I wish you'd go, Max."

But Max was not one to take orders easily. In a second, he had closed the distance between them. Samantha could not move as he took hold of her shoulders. His breath was warm on her face, and her heart was beating so hard suddenly that she wondered if he could hear it.

"It isn't true that you hate being in the same room as me." His voice was husky, his lips so close to hers that it was as if he was speaking right into her mouth.

"You're wrong! I can't stand it! And I can't stand you, either, Max! Get your hands off me!"

He did nothing of the sort, so that Samantha felt very hot suddenly, as if her body was in the grip of a high fever. Later, she would wonder why she hadn't just stepped away from him, but at that moment she seemed incapable of it.

"You may think you hate me," Max said softly. "I won't try to argue with that—for now. But don't try telling me you don't feel something when we're together. We both feel it, Samantha. Every time I've come to pick up Annie, it's been there. That wild urge to kiss and cling and make love."

"Stop!" she whispered. "I don't want to hear this—any of it—don't you understand?"

Max moved even closer. "I understand—" his voice was very low now, and unbearably seductive "—that we're both hungry to tear off our clothes and jump into bed."

"No!" she shouted. "Get out, Max!"

One hand left her shoulder, cupping her face instead. "It's always been that way with us. That's why you're so frantic now. Be honest with yourself, admit it."

He was right, of course, and Samantha knew it. Despite her anger, there had always been a part of her, that primitive part in the very core of her being, which had yearned to be in his arms every time he'd come to the apartment. *But she could not let him know it.*

What about Edna? She was about ask the question, but at that moment Max began to kiss her.

His kisses were hard and sweet and passionate, just as she remembered them. But there was an extra quality as well, an intensity that was unfamiliar, as if Max was making up for lost time. And wasn't *that* ridiculous!—the thought came to her grimly. Max had all the kissing he wanted, though from someone else.

She was about to pull away from him, when his tongue inserted itself between her lips. As he began to explore the inner recesses of her mouth, a hot tide of desire flooded through her, and then she was kissing him back, without thought, and with an abandon that she would remember with hot embarrassment later.

But for now there was only Max, only the vibrant body that she had missed so much in the time they had been apart. His hands were on her back now, and then moving lower to her hips, sliding over them in a sensuously caressing movement that drove Samantha almost to the brink of insanity.

She wasn't thinking as her hands lifted to clasp his neck and her fingers buried themselves in his thick, dark hair. All she wanted was to be close to him; she felt as if she couldn't get close enough. Oh, but she had missed him!

She heard his muffled groan against her mouth. And then he lifted his head and looked down at her. His eyes, normally dark brown, were almost black with desire.

"I want to make love to you." His voice was low and husky.

In an instant, something tightened inside her. She wanted it, too: God, how she wanted it! But something made her say, "Someone could see us."

"Annie's with Helen. And we'll lock the door."

Samantha hesitated, also yearning with every part of her being to make love. In this room that she had once shared with Max, the passionate desire that had once been so much a part of her life came rushing back, like a river in full flood.

"Besides," he reminded her, laughing softly, "we still have a license."

She was tempted, so terribly tempted to let him make love to her. Fortunately, at the last moment, reality struck. Summoning the willpower that seemed on the point of deserting her, she said, "As if the lack of a license—not to mention a vow to remain faithful to your wife—has ever stood in the way of doing anything you wanted."

"Samantha…" he began, his arms tightening around her.

She felt weak and a little giddy, wanting to give in to him, and knowing at the same time that she had to stand her ground.

"No, Max."

"Samantha, please. I know you'll—"

"Mommy! Daddy!" a voice shouted ecstatically.

They both turned to look at Annie, standing in the doorway, her small face radiant with joy. "You're kissing!"

"I thought you were with Helen," said her father.

"I was looking for you."

"Good thing, too," her mother murmured under her breath.

Max said a little raggedly, "Hey, Annie, Helen couldn't wait to see you again—why don't you stay with her a bit longer? Mommy and I will be with you soon."

"No." Samantha had recovered some of her composure. She made herself look at Max. "I think I should unpack before I do anything else."

"*Anything* else?" He met her gaze directly, his voice heavy with meaning.

"You heard me, Max."

A little hand tugged at his. "Daddy. Can we go play?"

Max took her hand. "Sure we can, princess."

At the door, he turned. "Later, then?"

Samantha expelled a breath. "Never."

Max slanted her a look. "Meaning you've changed your mind?"

"Your legal brain was always quick to grasp a concept."

"Sarcasm doesn't suit you, Samantha."

Samantha shrugged. "So you told me last time we met," she said. And this time it was her turn to grin at him.

The sound of laughter came through the open window. Dumping an armful of clothes on the bed, Samantha walked over to it. Annie and Max were playing below her in the garden. Max was pushing the child around the lawn in a wheelbarrow, and judging by their laughter, they were having a great time. Once, Max teasingly tipped the handles so that Annie slid to the ground. The whole thing was softly done, and the little girl shrieked with delight. Her father picked her up, dusted her down gently, and then put her back in the wheelbarrow. More laughter ensued as they went racing around the garden together.

A lump formed in Samantha's throat as she watched them play. Max had always been a good father, that was the one thing she had never been able to fault him with. She remembered his joy when Annie was born, the awe with which the big man had lifted the tiny infant from her crib, and looked down at her—as if he couldn't believe that he had helped create this small and perfect being.

How she longed to go and join them now: the little girl who was the center of her world, and the man who even now, after the terrible thing he had done to her, was still the standard by which she measured all other men. But she would not go into the garden. Not yet. She would wait until Max was safely out of the way.

Grimly she turned away from the window. As she picked up her clothes from the bed and began to hang them in the closet, she knew she would have to make a determined effort to remain detached from Max. At the same time, she understood that this wouldn't be easy.

With all her heart, she wished that she could erase the memory of their kisses. Her body still burned with the fire of a familiar longing. She didn't even want to speculate what would have happened if Annie hadn't walked in on them when she did.

In the solitude of the lovely master bedroom, she was able—just—to tell herself that in the end she wouldn't have allowed Max to make love to her. Yet the gnawing hunger deep in her loins told a different story. She had wanted, with every nerve and fiber of her being, to make wild and passionate love with Max.

All the more reason to keep her distance from him. If all she wanted from Max was sex, it was clearly hers for the taking. What would never be hers again, and what she craved more than anything else, was his love and commitment; without those, nothing else made sense. But Max's affair with Edna had put an end to their marriage, so that the divorce was now just a matter of time. Since she had no intention of letting him use or humiliate her ever again, it was important that she make him understand that lovemaking was a thing of the past.

Working more quickly now, she restored some order to the room. When her clothes were all put away in the mirrored closets, she unpacked her few toiletries and cosmetics, and put in place the photos of her family and the cherished objects that were an intimate part of her personal life.

Max had brought two more cases from the car and put them in Annie's room. It didn't take very long to unpack the child's clothes and toys. Looking around the pink-walled room, Samantha thought how different it was from Annie's tiny room in the apartment they had just left. In her father's house, Annie was indeed a princess; in her mother's home, she was an ordinary little girl. A girl who would grow up to be a fairly wealthy woman, thanks to her grandfather's inheritance.

With the suitcases unpacked, Samantha decided to take a shower. She was sitting at her dressing table, combing hair that was almost dry, when a familiar voice said, "Ready for dinner?"

Turning, she looked at Max and Annie standing in the doorway. Two pairs of eyes, the same color and shape; without any doubt the eyes of a father and daughter.

"I hadn't realized the time…"

"Guess you were busy." Max looked around the room. "It's as if you were never gone, Samantha. Everything's the same as it used to be."

"Nothing is the same. I did go, and I will again." Her voice shook.

"Do we have to, Mommy?" Annie wailed.

Swept with sudden guilt, Samantha looked down at the child, realizing that the emotions Max had aroused in her had made her forget that Annie was listening to everything her parents said. Not that Annie would be able to make any sense of undercurrents and double meanings, of things hinted at rather than spelled out.

"Daddy and I had such fun in the garden," Annie said.

"I know you did, honey. I saw you playing."

"Can't we stay here forever, Mommy? Please, Mommy, can't we stay?"

Over Annie's head, Samantha's eyes met Max's. One dark eyebrow lifted deliberately. He was not going to make this easy for her, she realized grimly. Stupid of her to have expected anything else of him.

She took Annie's hands. "We'll be here a long time, honey."

"Forever, Mommy?"

It was difficult to harden herself against the hope in Annie's voice and face. "Not forever, but quite a long time."

This time she met Max's eyes steadily. "Why don't you and Annie go to the table, and I'll join you in a few minutes." Unspoken in her expression, were the words, "And change the subject, Max."

Sitting together, the three of them around the mahogany dining-room table, eating the delicious meal Helen had prepared—including the fried chicken that was one of Annie's favorites—it was indeed as if Samantha and Annie had never been away. Everything was so wrenchingly familiar.

Unhappily Samantha looked at her child, her small face alive with interest as her father told her a story. When the time came, would she have to drag the little girl forcibly back to Manhattan? Perhaps the best she could hope for was that one day, when Annie was very much older, she would understand that her mother had only been thinking of her future when she'd brought her back to this house for six months.

"A magician, Max."

He looked at her quizzically. "Am I supposed to know what you're talking about?"

They were sitting on the patio, a spacious area leading off from the living room, with that wonderful view over the water. They had finished dinner a while ago, and Max had insisted on helping Samantha put Annie to bed.

It had been a long day for the little girl, but despite her obvious weariness, Annie had placed the proverbial matchsticks beneath her eyelids in an attempt to delay her bedtime for as long as she could. An indulgent Max had agreed to read her one story after another, until Annie's eyes had closed of their own accord. Samantha had drawn the blanket over her shoulders, and then bent to kiss her. On the other side of the bed, Max kissed her, too. And again, Samantha had grieved for the family they had once been.

She had been about to go to her room, when Max stopped her. Helen had left a thermos of coffee on the patio, he told her. Sit down and have a cup together, he suggested; and then, if she was really as tired as she said, he wouldn't try to keep her from going to bed.

"You're a magician," Samantha said. "Pulling out every one of your tricks."

Max laughed, the sound low and vital on the silent air. "Are you telling me I bring rabbits out of hats?"

Samantha leaned forward in her chair. "That's exactly what you do! Only your rabbits are irresistible temptations for small, impressionable girls."

She hadn't realized how close Max was to her, until he reached out and touched her hand. "Do I detect a note of bitterness?"

Samantha suppressed a shiver as she withdrew her hand. She was horrified that the skin burned where their hands had touched. This was how it had been between them when they had first met, when she had felt that she would be scorched by the flames of their mutual passion. But all that—the whirlwind courtship, the romantic honeymoon, the sense of love lasting forever—had happened in another world, in another time.

She was five years older now; twenty-five, disillusioned, skeptical, wise to the fact that the man she had thought she would always love was just playing games with her. *It made no sense at all that her emotions were as raw and as vital as they had been at the beginning.*

"True magicians know how to hide the way they do their tricks." Her voice was tight with tension as well as a treacherous longing. "But you're so transparent, Max—not to Annie, she's taken in completely—but to me. I see exactly what you're doing."

"You *are* bitter," he said softly.

"Do you wonder? I told you earlier that you'll never have custody of our child."

"I'm not planning a fight, Samantha."

"No, you're much too subtle for that. Seduction is your favored way. Make things so damned wonderful for Annie that she'll never want to leave. In six months she'll be *begging* not to leave. I don't have the money nor the resources to beat you at this game, Max."

In the soft glow of the patio light, his eyes were suddenly hooded. "And if she did want to stay—would that be so terrible?"

In an instant, Samantha was on her feet. "*Terrible?* Yes, Max, it would be terrible! I will never let you take my child away from me!"

"I told you—I don't plan a fight."

Samantha's hands clenched tightly at her sides, her nails digging painfully into the soft skin of her palms. "Your tactics are far more dangerous. You're making certain Annie will want to stay."

"You might want to stay, too—have you thought that?" His voice was so odd.

Samantha's legs were suddenly weak. She sat down again slowly. "That's ridiculous..."

"Is it? Remember, we're supposed to be making another attempt at marriage."

Samantha closed her eyes briefly. The picture that appeared behind her lids was tantalizing beyond belief, and just as unrealistic. She could only hope that Max hadn't registered the moment of weakness. Yet she knew that very little ever escaped him; in part, this was what made him such an excellent lawyer.

Her eyes snapped open. "We both know that's impossible. Your father meant well, Max, but he didn't know about Edna." The absurdity of the words struck her a moment after they had left her lips. "On second thought, he must have known. She's your woman after all."

"Is she?" Max drawled.

"Unless you've double-crossed her as well, and gone on to a third woman. I guess that's entirely possible."

Max laughed. "And I guess I should be flattered, but don't you think you're overestimating my sex appeal?"

Nobody—*no woman*—could ever overestimate that.

Max's sexuality was a raw and virile quality that clung to him like a second skin. His expensive shirts and suits couldn't mask the sheer animal vitality that emanated from him at all times. It was very easy to understand why Edna had been drawn to him. Even now, when Samantha was so angry with him, the urge to be close to him was almost irresistible. But for the sake of her sanity, she had to find a way of resisting—now and for the next six months.

Abruptly she asked, "Where has Edna been all day anyway?"

His reply was laconic.

"I have no idea."

"At least she had the sense to keep away. I meant what I said, Max—if you flaunt her in front of Annie, we'll be out of here in an instant."

"I would never hurt Annie."

"And I won't be humiliated. Once was more than enough. I can't stop you from seeing your mistress, but I won't have her anywhere near me nor my child."

"Why won't you let me talk to you about Edna?" Max's voice was hard.

"Because there's nothing to say."

"You're wrong, Samantha."

"Now you're insulting my intelligence. I know what I saw. And I know I wasn't dreaming. Do you honestly think I can ever forget, Max? You and Edna in that bed, wrapped in each other's arms?"

The memory was as vivid as ever, just as the pain that came with remembering never seemed to grow less. Samantha could not imagine how she could cope with seeing Max and Edna together again.

"Things aren't always what they seem, Samantha."

"I agree, but that doesn't apply in this instance. Maybe I'm naive, Max, but in my world, when a man and a woman are in bed together, it means only one thing."

"You believe they must be making love."

Samantha sensed a trap. "That's right—or at least about to be making love," she said crisply, covering all her bases. "Bottom line, Max—I don't want to see Edna."

"Never?"

"Never," she echoed feelingly. "It isn't too much to ask."

"You know as well as I do, that I can't guarantee anything. We work together after all. But I won't humiliate you, Samantha."

She stared at him suspiciously. "Is that a promise?"

"Let's say it's the best answer I can give you." Max's grin was infuriating.

It wasn't the answer she wanted, but for now it was as much as she would probably hope to get from him, Samantha realized.

CHAPTER THREE

"SAMANTHA..."

Lying beneath the blanket, she stirred. Her name had been spoken so softly, just the way she heard it so often in the mornings, in those moments before she woke up. It was a few seconds before she realized that this time she was not dreaming.

She heard Max's footsteps as he came to the bed, and sensed him standing beside her. Desire flamed quickly to life as she felt the warmth of his body reaching to hers. In the half state between sleeping and waking, she was about to lift her arms to him. And then she remembered the reason for her presence in the house. Making herself lie very still, she managed to keep her breathing slow and unhurried. With any luck, Max would believe she was asleep, and go.

He did just that. Minutes later, Samantha heard the back door of the house close, and then the sound of his car driving away.

She wondered whether he had been taken in by her act. What she did know was that she would not sleep again. She was hungry with the desire to be in his arms—hunger like a physical ache, hunger that wouldn't go away quickly.

And what of Max? He was on his way to the station, from where he would take the train into Manhattan, blissfully unaware of the havoc he had caused. By now, his mind would be occupied by thoughts of whatever case he was working on; if he had experienced any physical yearnings whatsoever, they would be forgotten the moment he saw Edna.

Edna... But she could not let herself brood about the woman. Could not keep thinking about her every day. There were so many other things to occupy her mind. Pushing aside the blanket, she got out of bed.

When she walked into Annie's room a little while later, the child was just waking. Flinging her arms around her mother's neck, she shouted, "We're still here!"

"Where did you think we'd be, honey?" Samantha made herself smile down at her.

"In the apartment." Annie's expression was suddenly so wistful, that Samantha felt her heart wrench.

Hugging the little girl tightly, she leaned her cheek against Annie's soft tousled hair. "We're here now, Annie. Are you hungry, honey?"

"Yes!"

"How about we go to the kitchen and I'll make you some breakfast?"

Annie wriggled away from her. "Afterward, can I play with Daddy?"

"Daddy's gone to work."

"Will he come back again?"

How insecure the little girl was, Samantha thought sadly. And with good reason. Aloud, she said, "Yes, Annie, he will. Let's go downstairs now. Shall I make you some pancakes?"

Squealing with pleasure, the child jumped out of bed in an instant, and ran ahead of Samantha down the stairs. A smiling Helen was in the kitchen. The kitchen was warm, and the air was filled with the delicious aroma of recent baking.

"My favorite little girl!" Helen cried, holding out her arms to Annie. "Say, pet, do you like muffins? I hope you do, because I just baked a whole batch, especially for you. Blueberry muffins and a glass of milk. How does that sound, Annie?"

Her mother's pancakes forgotten, a rapturous Annie shouted, "Wow!"

Helen turned to Samantha. "And a muffin and coffee for you, Mrs. Anderson?"

Mrs. Anderson... Even though she had decided to retain her married name for the time being, on the lips of the housekeeper it sounded a little odd to Samantha after all this time. Without wanting to go into the details of the charade, she just smiled and said, "Sounds wonderful. Oh, and Helen, please call me Samantha."

She was at the cupboard, taking out two plates, when Helen came up behind her and took them from her hand. "You don't have to do that."

Samantha was taken aback, and more than a little frustrated. "Thanks, Helen, but I want to. I'm used to it—I've been taking care of myself all the time I was away."

"You're back now, and this is my job," the other woman said simply. She looked across the kitchen at Annie, before adding quietly, "We're all so glad you're here. Mr. Anderson especially."

Mr. Anderson had done very well without her, Samantha thought grimly. Helen could hardly be unaware of Edna's role in his life. If asked, she might even fill her in on some of the details. It would not surprise her if the other woman spent many a night here. Not that she had seen any evidence of it so far, but then it made sense that Edna would have removed her possessions before Samantha's return. Yet Samantha knew better than to ask Helen about Edna. If Max thought she was discussing his private life with the housekeeper, there would be hell to pay.

By midmorning she was feeling restless. After living alone for so long, Samantha had become accustomed to doing things her own way. From the time the alarm clock woke her at dawn, the day moved to a certain routine. On weekdays, there was always the rush to get herself and

Annie ready, so that she could take the little girl to her kindergarten, and still get to work on time. Saturdays and Sundays were programmed differently: after the grocery shopping and the household chores had been taken care of, and if Max was not expected to pick up Annie, Samantha would take her daughter to parks or the zoo, or to one of the many festivals and parades taking place in and around Manhattan. One way or another, the days were full. After less than twenty-four hours, she already knew that things were going to be very different here.

"I'm going to be working," she announced that evening.

Max glowered at her over his coffee. Once again, Samantha had decided to wait until Annie was in bed before broaching the subject that had been on her mind all that day.

"I thought you'd taken leave of absence."

"I did. But I still want to work. Not in Manhattan. Hopefully I can find a job nearby."

"Full-time?" His voice was hard.

"Part-time."

"I don't like it, Samantha."

"I'm sorry, Max, but I'm working anyway."

"What about Annie?" There was an ominous look in his eyes.

"She'll be just fine. I had a call from a junior kindergarten this morning. Seems you were in touch with them before we got here?"

"I thought she might miss being with other children," Max said.

"She would. Annie is so sociable, she adores being with other kids. I'll need to take a look at the place first, Max. If I like it... They can take her right away. Which leaves my mornings free."

Max put his cup firmly down on the table. "I'm sure you could find something to occupy your time."

Remembering that he had always been something of an old-fashioned husband where women and independence were concerned, his resistance didn't surprise Samantha. She held his eyes, ignoring the opposition she glimpsed there. "Like what?" she challenged.

Max frowned. "Whatever women do in their spare time. Gallery-hopping? Coffee with friends? Aerobics?"

Samantha couldn't help smiling. "You're talking about quite a select set of women. Not the real world, Max. The world in which women have careers, usually because they need to, but even when they don't. If I've learned anything in the time I've been away, it's that."

"Granted. But you're part of that select set."

"I used to be."

He looked at her, his eyes thoughtful. "Anything wrong with gallery-hopping and aerobics?"

"Not a thing. Great activities—ones I used to enjoy. And will again when I have the time for them. But they're not for me right now, Max."

"You could always shop," he suggested after a moment.

"I have all I need, and so does Annie. Besides, my budget doesn't run to unnecessary shopping."

Max's expression became tight, a little dangerous. "I've never denied you a thing," he said mutinously. "It's been your choice to send back my checks."

"I didn't want your money, I don't want it now, either. That hasn't changed."

"Nonsense," he said succinctly.

Samantha felt her blood start to boil. "Don't put me down, Max. I won't stand for it."

"I'm not trying to put you down, Samantha. But I've never understood why you refused to accept support from me. I *wanted* you to have it."

Samantha put down her own cup with a slight bang.

"You still don't get it, do you, Max? After what happened, I want nothing to do with you or your money."

He looked more than a little irritated. "Be that as it may, there's no *need* for you to work."

"I want to," she said stubbornly.

He seized her wrist. "It was one thing for you to be independent while we were apart, but now that we're back together I'll be providing for you and Annie. And don't try arguing me out of it, Samantha." His tone was harsh.

There was nothing even remotely loverlike in the way he was holding her, yet Samantha could not stop the shiver that shot from her hand all the way up her arm. Forcing herself to concentrate, she said, "We'll only be together six months. And I am going to work—whether you like it or not, Max."

Clearly Max did not share her physical reaction. If anything, he looked even more frustrated. "Do you think I'd take money for rent or food? Do you? If so, you can think again."

Pulling her hand out of his—a feat that took more strength than Samantha would have imagined—she threw him a look of pure challenge. "Maybe not rent and food. But I've got used to being independent. It costs money to live, and I can't just stop working."

"You don't need the money. For God's sake, Samantha, what does it take to make you understand?" His voice had an edge to it, as if he was trying very hard to maintain his composure.

"*You* don't understand, Max. Granted, being here gives me a bit of a respite—I'll be able to save a lot of what I earn. But it will be very nice to have a bit of a nest egg put by for when Annie and I are on our own again."

"What about Annie?" he demanded. "What happens to her when you're working?"

"I've told you—she'll be at her kindergarten in the

mornings, and I'll be with her in the afternoons. If I have to work a bit late—and I won't take a job where that's likely to happen often—Helen says she'll be happy to take care of her.''

''You have all the answers, don't you?'' He threw the words at her harshly.

Once, Samantha might have been intimidated by his attitude, but no longer. ''Annie won't be neglected,'' she said quietly, ''any more than she was neglected when we were alone in Manhattan together.''

Max stared at her somberly. His lips were tight, his jawline hard. Frustration was evident in every line of the handsome face, and Samantha didn't care in the least. There was a time—in another world it seemed now—when she had done everything she could to please him, even when she knew he was being unreasonable. It gave her no small sense of satisfaction to realize that she no longer depended on Max's approval.

''You really do have all the answers,'' he muttered.

She slanted him a mischievous grin. ''Some of them.''

''Only some?'' His tone was sarcastic.

''The ones that matter to me.''

He searched her face, his gaze lingering quite deliberately on her lips. ''I used to think I knew you, Samantha. Now I don't know what to make of you.''

''Are you saying I'm a woman of mystery?''

''In some ways.''

''I think I like that.''

Without warning, Max reached for her hands and drew her to her feet. ''I like it, too,'' he said unexpectedly.

''Good Lord!'' Samantha exclaimed in surprise.

''Even though I don't like a damn thing you're saying.''

He was going to kiss her, Samantha thought wildly, and she wanted him to. But something made her draw back.

She tilted her head so that she could look at him. "Does this mean you don't mind me working?"

"I mind very much."

She tried, unsuccessfully, to push away from him. "Max—"

"But you've made up your mind, and there doesn't seem any point going on about it."

"Well!" She stared up at him, trying to hide her astonishment. After a moment, she said, "I think I'll go to my room."

His arms went around her. He was so close to her now that even though their bodies weren't actually touching, she could feel his warmth. "Not so fast."

Her heart began to race. "You said there was no point going on about it. I only stayed out here to talk."

His hands moved over her back. "You've won, Samantha—don't you understand? I don't like the thought you'll be working, that hasn't changed. But right now I want to kiss you."

"Max..." she said, not at all convincingly.

"Have you any idea how sexy you are? All those things you were saying—I was angry, yes. But you were also making me very excited."

And then he was kissing her, with all the hunger and passion of the previous day. And after a few seconds she was kissing him, too—despite the fact that on the edge of her mind a small voice reminded her she had decided not to.

When they moved apart to draw breath, Samantha managed to ask, "Whatever will Edna say?"

"She has nothing to do with it," Max said roughly.

He was reaching for her once more, but Samantha had regained some of the reality she had temporarily lost. "Doesn't she?" Her voice was tight with tension.

"You know damn well she doesn't! If you don't, you should."

"I know nothing of the kind," Samantha countered hotly. "Unless of course you're cheating on her as well?"

"We talked about this yesterday." Max was still breathing hard.

"But you didn't give me an answer." Taking a step backward, she said, "Well, are you? Cheating on her?"

Max was just far enough from her now that Samantha could see his eyes glitter. "Don't tell me you're concerned about Edna."

"I can't bear the woman."

"Then why the question?"

"Curiosity."

"Sure that's all it is?"

"Absolutely! We'll be divorced soon, so what else could it be at this point?"

A little roughly, Max said, "You're still my wife, Samantha."

She forced a small laugh. "So you keep reminding me."

"I'd like to go on reminding you," Max said, trying to reach for her once more.

Samantha managed—somehow—to resist him. "I'm not interested, Max."

"You were interested a few minutes ago. More than a little interested," he said mockingly.

Samantha swallowed hard. "You could say I've come to my senses—I'm not interested now."

"You're lying, Samantha."

"You keep flattering yourself, Max."

But she was lying—she knew that only too well as she walked away from him. As she closed the door of her bedroom, her body throbbed with unfulfilled desire.

Samantha liked kindergarten the moment she saw it. It was small, yet spacious and bright, with pictures and posters on the walls, shelves filled with toys and three friendly teachers who made Annie welcome. Sociable Annie immediately wanted to join in the activities of her new group.

With the morning to herself, and nothing in particular to do—she had no intention of interfering with Helen's very capable handling of the household—Samantha began to look for a job. Three days passed before she walked into the office of Hugh and Martin Rowland, architects who were also brothers. The job they offered her seemed tailor-made to her requirements.

Max was home earlier than usual that evening. He had phoned some time during the afternoon and told Helen not to prepare supper. After changing into jeans and a T-shirt, he told Samantha and Annie that he was taking them out to eat. The little girl was ecstatic when the car entered the parking lot of a fast-food restaurant.

"Not quite your usual style," Samantha commented dryly, as they walked inside.

Max flashed her a sparkling grin. "It's been so long since we've been out together—what do you remember of my style?"

She grinned back at him. "Entrecôte steak and a bottle of wine. Served by candlelight and accompanied by soft music. Maître d' hovering at your shoulder."

"Did you like my style?"

His hand was on her arm as they walked to a table in a corner. A casual touch, yet as usual, Samantha's skin burned even after the contact was broken.

"You made a girl feel special," she said lightly.

"Oh, yes?" he drawled suggestively. "Well, tonight I want to make another girl feel special. A younger girl." He looked down at Annie. "What would you like, princess? Hamburger? French fries? Ice cream? Maybe a bit of everything?"

"Yeah!" Annie exclaimed rapturously, at the same time as her mother said, "Take it easy, Max. We don't want to give her a tummy-ache."

"And you, Samantha—what will you have?"

"Why don't you choose?" she suggested.

"I thought I was in the company of an independent woman," he teased.

"You are." She grinned at him. "But she does have her off moments sometimes."

Max grinned back at her, then took Annie's hand. "Tell you what, princess, why don't you come with me, and we'll order together?"

"Yeah!" Annie said again.

Samantha watched them walking away, Max looking dynamic in his tight-fitting jeans. Dressed in casual clothes, nobody would take him for a lawyer who was fast making a name for himself with his courtroom brilliance. With that brand of raw and virile sexiness that clung to him at all times, he could as well be a cowboy or a movie star.

Every woman in the place must be green with envy that Max was her man, she thought. Except that he *wasn't* her man—strange, how she had to keep reminding herself of that fact. Strange, too, that his closeness still had the power to inflame her. With all her heart, she wished that she wasn't quite so aware of him.

They came back to the table, Max carrying the tray with their food, laughing as he joked with Annie. Samantha wondered how he would take her news.

"Look what we got, Mommy!" Annie shouted.

"Hope it's what you want," Max said, putting the tray down on the table. "You used to enjoy the soft-serve ice cream."

"Still do." She didn't tell him that the choice of food

was unimportant: what mattered was being together as a family.

If only she didn't love Max so much. She had been so certain, after his betrayal, that her love for him had died. It hadn't. She doubted now it ever would. In the circumstances, this was no cause for joy.

She ate the ice cream slowly. Across the table from her, Annie dug into her French fries with such abandon, that one would have thought it was ages since her last meal.

Beside Samantha, sat Max...so close to her that she felt the length of a thigh against her leg. Now and then he moved—deliberately, she was sure—and the feel of the hard muscles rubbing against her set up a quivering that was difficult to control.

"You're hardly eating," Max said at last.

She looked up. "I'm not all that hungry."

"Something on your mind, Samantha?" The question was casually asked, but the watchful eyes were anything but casual.

She put down her spoon. "I found a job."

After a silence, Max said, "Didn't take you long."

"Not very long, no."

"Care to tell me about it?"

She shrugged. "If you're interested."

"Everything about you interests me, Samantha," he drawled, at the same time as a hard thigh moved against her once more.

Her nerves were so raw that she would have liked to increase the distance between them, but the placement of the seats made that impossible.

Softly, so that Annie wouldn't hear him, Max said, "I don't bite. Now tell me about the job."

Samantha lifted her chin at him. "I'm going to be working for two brothers. Architects by the name of Rowland."

"Never heard of them."

"Nice men."

"Are they?" A slight edge to his tone.

Samantha darted him a mischievous look. "Very nice, indeed."

"Good," he said curtly. "And your duties?"

"Something of a girl Friday. They're both quite young, not yet well-established, and they seem to need someone who can do a bit of everything. I'll be a combination receptionist/secretary. They said that in time they might even teach me some drafting. It sounds like a perfect job, Max." She looked at him. "Pity I won't be able to work there more than a few months."

When Max ignored the last words, Samantha felt a small stab of disappointment—only to chide herself a second later for expecting anything more from him.

"How about your working hours?" His voice was hard.

"Mornings only," she told him. "Four mornings a week at the start—and I get to choose the days. I'll be able to spend the afternoons with Annie. Exactly the kind of job I was looking for."

Max was silent for so long that Samantha looked at him challengingly. "Nothing to say?" she asked at last, tartly.

"Just one thing."

Samantha tensed. Was it possible that Max would try to put a spoke in her plans? She would stand up to him if he tried! She flinched as a warm hand reached unexpectedly for her chin, turning her face toward him.

"Max…?"

"Why so startled?" he asked, obviously amused.

"You took me by surprise," she muttered.

But they both knew it was more than that. His hand still held her chin, and now his thumb began to stroke slowly up and down her face in a movement that was so erotic that Samantha's breath grew shallow.

Unsteadily she murmured, "Annie..."

Quietly Max said, "Is totally absorbed in her French fries. Besides, why would she think there was anything wrong with her father touching her mother?"

Samantha forced herself to meet Max's eyes. "She wouldn't—just as she wouldn't understand about Edna...she's too young for that."

"She doesn't have to."

"Not yet." They were both speaking quietly. "Take your hand away, Max." When he did so, she went on, "You had a comment about the job?"

"A condition, actually."

She sent him another challenging look. "You've no right to make conditions, Max."

His answering look was wicked. "You haven't heard it yet."

"Well?"

"Dinner for two at the restaurant of my choice, with your first salary check."

Samantha was swept with sudden happiness. "It's a deal!"

"Entrecôte steak and a bottle of wine?"

"And a decadent dessert to finish the meal."

"Will your salary run to that?"

"Definitely!"

They looked at each other and laughed, and it was another one of those precious moments that had been missing for too long from Samantha's life.

And then, almost in the same second, they looked at Annie, and laughed again. The little girl's face and hands were covered with ketchup. She was having a wonderful time, and it was evident that she hadn't heard one word of her parents' conversation.

"You're a bit of a mess," her father said, still laughing. "Maybe your mother will clean you up while I go and get you an ice cream?"

By the time Max returned with a cone, Samantha had used up a whole wad of napkins, and Annie was relatively clean again. Both parents concentrated on the child now, taking it in turns to tell jokes and stories.

Annie was enjoying herself immensely, but Samantha was enjoying herself even more. For this one evening, the three of them were a family, and it didn't seem important that they were living an illusion.

She was on her way to bed, when Max stopped her. "By the way, Charles and Nora Langley are going to be hosting a cocktail party for the firm one of these days."

Charles Langley was one of the founding members of Max's law firm. "What does that have to do with me?" Samantha asked.

"Everything, since you'll be coming with me." And as she stared at him, "Is there a problem with that?"

As if she really needed to spell it out for him, Samantha thought grimly. Edna was an associate of the firm, and Max knew, without being told, that Samantha had no wish to meet the other woman.

"Count me out, Max."

"I want you to come, Samantha. All the other spouses will be there."

"Since I'm only technically your spouse, that lets me off the hook," she said crisply.

"Nothing technical about it—especially since we've decided to put our divorce on hold for the moment." His voice was equally crisp. "It's an important affair, partners only, and I want you to be there."

She looked at him. "Partners only?"

"Correct."

The law firm was big, with close to fifty partners, as well as many associates. Edna was an associate.

"I still don't think I should go..."

"I've already said you'll be there."

Samantha shook her head indignantly. "How could you, Max? You had absolutely no right to speak on my behalf. I'm sorry, but you'll just have to find a way of excusing my absence."

Closing the distance between them, Max took hold of her shoulders. "Think how it will look if I arrive without you," he said quietly.

Samantha was shocked. "Are you saying our charade of a marriage is common knowledge?"

"Nobody knows it's a charade, but people do know we're together again. I couldn't keep it a secret."

"And they all know about your father's will?" she asked curiously.

"Only Stan Manson knows. He's Dad's executor. Obviously he's familiar with the conditions of the will."

Samantha remembered Stan Manson: semiretired, and a lifelong friend of William Anderson's.

"Stan knows what Dad was trying to achieve when he put in that condition. I believe he'd take it badly if he thought we were just living a sham, and not making an honest attempt to fix our relationship."

Samantha moved out of Max's hands. She had to think, and she couldn't do that when his sexiness was distracting her.

"It seems there's more to your father's will than I realized," she said at last, troubled. "I didn't realize other people were involved."

"Other people being Stan. What's the problem, Samantha? You came back for Annie's sake. That hasn't changed, has it?"

"No," she agreed abruptly. "It's the only reason I'm here. The *only* reason, Max."

"Having got that out of the way again—" his voice was sardonic "—what's your decision about the party?"

But she wasn't ready to give him an answer.

What she did know was that the sense of the walls closing in that she'd experienced before, was back in full force.

CHAPTER FOUR

MAX burst out laughing. "Tweedledum and Tweedledee?"

"That's right. Hugh and Martin. Two little men, with apple-cheeked faces and a million freckles. Identical, though they're not twins. I wish you could see them, Max—they're an absolute riot. I adore them both."

Max took a sip of wine. Putting down the glass, he said, "So you're really enjoying your work there?"

"I love it! The money is good, and that's great. But more than that, my mind is challenged and I'm developing a real sense of self-worth." Her eyes met his. "Have you any idea how important that is to me?"

"Why don't you tell me?"

Samantha played with the stem of her own wineglass, twirling it in her fingers a few moments. "It's the first time I'm actually putting this into words," she said at last. "Remember how old I was when we were married?"

"How could I forget? It was your twentieth birthday."

"That's right. You were ten years older. A lawyer already on the brink of a great career. Smarter and more mature than me, wise in the ways of the world. From one day to the next, my life changed. Sure, I had lost my parents, but my grandparents were always there for me. And there was my sister. Until Dorothy got married, we had each other."

"Not unlike my own background in some ways," Max said.

Samantha was quiet a moment. She knew Max was thinking of his own sister, Melissa—but this was not the moment to get on to that particular subject.

"From being a carefree girl," she went on, "with little more on my mind than enjoying myself, suddenly I was a married woman, with a big house to run, clients and other lawyers to entertain and a husband who was far more sophisticated than I'd realized. Have you any idea how I felt, Max?"

His eyes had not moved from her face while she spoke, and it was obvious he was listening intently. "I thought you were in love with me."

"I was! Head over heels in love! You came into my life, Max—at the beach party, remember?—and I couldn't believe you were interested in me."

"Interested?" He gave a rough laugh. "There you were, playing volleyball with a bunch of boys who were all more interested in you than in the ball. And I couldn't blame them. You were gorgeous. Your hair was tumbling around your face, and your laughter sounded like music. The ball got away from you, and rolled my way. I picked it up, and as you took it from me, I saw your eyes for the first time. They were so big, Samantha, green and sparkling, and when you smiled and said thanks, I felt as if I'd been struck right in the heart. I knew I could live with those eyes all my life, and I asked you to have dinner with me." He paused, and smiled at her. "The rest, as they say, is history."

Samantha shot him a spirited look. "Pity the history didn't end there."

"Point taken." His lips were tight suddenly, his eyes hooded. "But you were telling me about your job, and why it's so important to you. I want to hear more about it."

"The long answer or the short one?" she asked after a moment.

"As long as it takes."

"Okay, here it is. When I left you, I had to learn to be independent. Quickly. I'm not saying being a single mother is fun—it isn't. Too little money, difficult to make ends meet, too many responsibilities. For the moment, at least, I don't have those same responsibilities, and I can't say that isn't nice. But when I was on my own, hard as it was, I was my own person. And that felt good, Max. Really good.''

Her eyes sparkled as she talked, so that the watching man thought he had never seen her looking quite so alive, so lovely—and so very sexy. He yearned, quite desperately, to carry her out of the restaurant, and take her to bed. He could have done it with the old Samantha. Had done it more than once. There had been meals when the sparks between them had flamed with such energy that they had left the food on their plates and raced home, shedding their clothes en route to the bedroom. But the beautiful woman sitting across the table from him was the new Samantha, and he had to earn her trust—and her love—before he could suggest anything quite so extreme.

Samantha only saw an inexplicable strangeness in the dark eyes. She wondered what Max was thinking. If he tried to change her mind about working, if he tried to put some obstacle in her way, she knew she would have to stand her ground.

"Do you understand, Max?" Her voice was a little tight.

"I think so." He smiled suddenly. "Tell me more about the brothers Tweedle."

Samantha expelled a small breath she'd hardly known she was holding. "They're fine architects—I know, because I've seen some of their work, actual buildings as well as work in progress. They're innovative and imaginative. And at the same time they are totally disorganized. You wouldn't believe the mess in that office. It's a wonder they ever find anything they're looking for. Books and papers everywhere, hardly an empty surface to work on."

"Until you arrived and brought some order into their lives."

"Right. You've no idea how grateful they are—which is why they insisted on giving me this huge check at the end of my first week."

"And which is why I'm being treated to this fantastic dinner." Max's smile had intensified, the wonderful smile that seemed to find its way straight into her heart every time she saw it.

It made her feel feminine and alive in a way she had not felt for so long.

The meal—tender beef medallions covered with succulent prawns, and served with small herbed potatoes—had indeed been fantastic. The whole evening had been special. Looking at Max across the flickering flame of the candle, Samantha felt a great surge of love, and yet also of sadness.

With every passing day, her feelings for Max seemed to grow stronger. He was not only the best-looking man she had ever met, but he was also the most vital. Certainly the sexiest. With every fiber of her being, she yearned to be a real part of his life again, to be his wife in every way.

But that could never be.

She had put down her knife and fork while she talked. Now she picked them up abruptly and cut into a piece of meat. But the meal seemed to have lost some of its taste.

"Why so grim suddenly?"

Samantha looked across the table at her soon-to-be ex-husband. "Grim?"

"For a while there you seemed to be having a good time. And then suddenly things changed. The way you attacked your food just now, I had the awful feeling that if you could, you would be plunging the knife into *me* rather than the meat."

"How dramatic," Samantha taunted.

"Am I wrong?"

"I'm too civilized for anything like that," she said shortly.

"Which is not to say you don't have uncivilized thoughts."

Involuntarily Samantha grinned. "Meaning I don't manage to hide them from you?"

And wouldn't that be something! Her beloved Max, knowing how deeply she felt about him. But he didn't know, he couldn't possibly. More than that, it was important he didn't. They would be divorced soon, the proceedings would get under way again once she left him. It was bad enough that her heart would break, she didn't want to be humiliated as well.

Max said cheerfully, "Hide your thoughts? Not for a moment. Don't you realize I know you almost as well as you know yourself?"

"Dangerous thought!" Samantha's eyes sparkled. "Especially if I'd really been thinking what you thought I was thinking. Not that I've said that I was."

"Nor that you weren't. Tell you what—" Max leaned across the table, and put his hand over one of hers "—why don't we call a truce?"

Heart beating very hard suddenly, Samantha said lightly, "Okay—for tonight."

Max's hand was warm and vital on hers, and a long shiver of desire went right through her body. His eyes were on her face, lingering on her lips, as caressingly as if he were kissing them.

"For tonight," he agreed at length. A moment passed, and then he added, his voice low with meaning, "The whole night, Samantha?"

As she snatched back her hand, her heart somersaulted inside her. "Just the evening," she said, a little bumpily.

"Why not make it the whole night?" No mistaking the seductiveness in his tone now.

It was an effort to remain still on her chair. "You're talking nonsense," she said faintly.

"Am I?" Max drawled.

"You know you are!"

"I'll tell you what I know, Samantha." His voice had become even more seductive. "You're still the most beautiful woman I've ever met. Sexy beyond belief. And I—"

"*Stop!*" She hurled the word at him.

"Why?"

"I can't bear it, that's why! Don't you understand, Max?"

"No, Samantha, I don't. All I know is, you used to enjoy sexy talk."

"Max—" A strangled cry.

It was his turn to interrupt her. "It's true, darling. We both know it."

She leaped from her chair. "*And don't call me darling!* You've no right to! Not any longer! We both know that, too."

Once more he reached for her hand, his fingers encircling her wrist this time. "Sit down," he said quietly, as hot flames shot up her arm.

"I can't!" She tried to pull her hand away from him, but his fingers were surprisingly strong. "Let me go, Max."

"Please sit, Samantha. We were having such a great evening. Don't let's spoil it now."

Aware of a few curious looks directed their way, Samantha did sit again. "*You* were spoiling it," she hissed at him.

"Sorry, I didn't think I was. Nor did I mean to upset you." Across his cheeks and around his eyes, the skin was tightly drawn. "Anyway, I've apologized. Now, let's go on with our dinner. I've been waiting for this evening since the day you started work.''

He was obviously trying to make the best of the situation, and after a moment Samantha tried to do the same. For a while they ate in silence. And then they began to talk once more.

Samantha told Max how well things were working out with Annie. Usually she was in time to pick her up from kindergarten, but there had been a day when she had needed to work a little later, and Helen had gone for the child. The housekeeper seemed only too happy to take care of Annie, and their affection was mutual.

They finished their entrées, and then the waiter returned with the dessert menu. Throwing calorie-counting to the winds, they decided to share a slice of cheesecake, and ordered two Irish coffees as well. They began to talk of other things—an art show, a festival in one of the parks, the upcoming wedding of a friend. They were talking easily now, even laughing together at a few shared memories. As they talked, it came to Samantha how natural this was, how the evening was like so many evenings in the past. It all seemed so *right*—and was yet so terribly wrong.

The waiter put the bill beside Max, and he lifted an eyebrow at Samantha. "Second thoughts about paying?"

"Certainly not!"

"We could go Dutch." She shook her head. "Will you let me pay for the wine?"

"What is this, Max? It was your idea that I treat you to dinner. Why are you changing your mind now?"

"Moment of weakness." He shot her a wicked grin. "Actually it's rather nice being treated. If you like, you can treat me again when you get your first raise."

Samantha reached for the bill. "I would say it's a deal, but I don't expect a raise in the next six months, and I won't be here after that."

If she expected him to argue the point, she was disappointed. "If you say so," was his only response.

Walking out of the restaurant, Samantha saw several women looking at Max. Funny, how she had forgotten the impact he had on other people. There was a time when she had gotten a real kick out of seeing the attention Max received wherever they went. It had always made her feel special, knowing that he could have attracted any number of women, and that she was the one he had fallen in love with. She hadn't dreamed then that Max would ever be unfaithful to her. She could only wonder now at her false sense of security.

It wasn't far from the restaurant back to the house. Samantha got out of the car at the front door, leaving Max to park it. She didn't wait for him as she went inside. Helen, watching television in the kitchen, said she had read to Annie for a while before putting her to bed. With a friendly good-night to Samantha, she left the kitchen.

Samantha went directly to Annie's room, where she bent over the sleeping child for a few seconds. Max hadn't come into the house yet when she went to her own room.

She was just starting to undress when she heard a knock. "Max...?" she said, and opened the door.

He just stood there in the open doorway, looking at her. His eyes moved over her face, down her throat, and on to her breasts, where the buttons of her blouse were already undone. The intensity of his gaze brought a hot flush to Samantha's cheeks.

"What are you doing here?" she asked, a little unsteadily.

"I thought you'd wait downstairs for me."

"Why would you think that?" Her voice shook. "It took you a while to come into the house."

His eyes were on her hips now. "There was something I had to see to in the garage."

Samantha made herself shrug. ''Well, anyway—I'm sure you didn't think I'd be waiting to kiss you good-night.''

''Exactly what I did expect,'' he drawled suggestively.

''Come on, Max!''

''We never had an evening out without making love afterward.''

Samantha began to tremble. ''If you think that's what's going to happen now, you're mistaken.''

''It's what we both want, darling.''

''Not true! And I asked you not to call me that.''

His hands went to her throat, his fingers resting lightly on the hollow at the base. ''Your pulse is so fast. Feels like it's beating right into my hands.

That was always a telltale sign, Samantha.''

He was right, of course—damn him! She could no more control her pulse than she could do anything about her breathing. If only she had thought to refasten her buttons before opening the door to him.

''Get out!'' she hissed.

''Quiet, darling, we don't want to wake Annie.'' With which he moved past her into the room.

''I'm warning you, Max,'' Samantha began, as he reached for her. ''If you make love to me now, you'll be forcing me—and I won't stand for that.''

''Forcing you?'' he drawled. ''You're lying, Samantha. Remember, that pulse of yours tells the truth even when your lips don't.''

He bent his head and brushed her throat with his tongue, so erotically that for a few moments Samantha could scarcely breathe.

When she thought she would faint with desire, he lifted his head. ''A kiss is all I'll ask from you—tonight.''

''Tonight?'' she echoed weakly.

He grinned at her. "A simple good-night kiss to seal a lovely evening."

But the kiss was anything but simple. The tantalizing exploration of her mouth, while at the same time his hands moved slowly over her hips, was so exciting that Samantha felt as if she would explode with excitement. Later, alone, she would admit to herself that if Max had tried to take her to bed, she wouldn't have been able to refuse him.

Yet now, after raising her to a pitch of desire, he was ready to leave her. *How could he do this to her?*

He was at the door when he turned back. "Nearly forgot. The party."

"Party…?" Samantha was dazed. She was trying very hard to control her trembling.

"The firm's party. I told you about it—remember? It's tomorrow, at the Langleys."

"I still don't think I should go…."

"Too late. I've said you'll be there."

"How could you, Max! I didn't say I'd come."

"I want you there, Samantha."

He was unyielding. Samantha had the odd feeling that if she didn't agree to go willingly, Max would find a way of luring her to the party anyway.

But still, there was something she had to know. "Max… Will Edna be there?"

"I remember telling you—partners only."

"You're certain?"

"Yes."

"How about Stan Manson?"

"He'll be there."

Stan Manson, who would think it suspicious if Max was at the party alone. Voice low, Samantha said, "Seems I have no option. I'll go, Max, but only for Annie's sake. To make sure there's no problem with her inheritance.''

Max gave a low wolf whistle as Samantha came down the stairs toward him. ''You look tremendous!''

She laughed at him. ''Flirt!''

''Seriously. You'll have every man at the party drooling over you. New dress, Samantha? I don't remember seeing it.''

''You haven't.''

In fact, she had gone shopping after work that day. With what was left of her first salary check, she had bought the prettiest dress she could find. Samantha couldn't remember when she had taken such care with her appearance. Her hair, which she normally wore brushed back behind her ears, now curled softly around her face, and she wore a little more makeup than usual. To complement the new outfit—a tight-fitting wine-red dress, floor-length, and with a slit that ran all the way up one thigh—she wore the antique silver earrings and matching necklace that Max had given her for their third anniversary.

She hadn't taken any of her jewelry when she left Max. But a few days ago she had found some of the things he had given her in a velvet-lined box in a drawer of her dressing table. Had he put them there purposely, thinking she would find them and use them? Or had they been there all the time? One way or another, the answer hadn't seemed to matter very much, since she didn't think she would ever wear any of Max's gifts again.

Until today, when she'd realized she would need all the confidence she could muster. All the legal partners would be at the party tonight, people she had not seen for close on a year. Samantha had no idea whether she would be met with curiosity or pity; perhaps a little of both, depending on how much people knew. The fact was, she would be better able to face scrutiny if she looked her best.

At the door of the Langleys' house, Samantha took an involuntary shuddering breath. As if he sensed her nervousness, Max took her hand.

"You look great," he said softly. "Everyone will be thrilled to see you again."

"Max..." she began uncertainly.

"Relax, Samantha. You'll do just fine. You may even enjoy the party—if you give yourself a chance."

She doubted he was right about that, but for her own sake she was going to do her best to present a confident appearance.

"Samantha—how nice!"

Nora Langley took her by the hand as they walked through the entrance hall and into the sumptuous living room of her house. Nora's husband, Charles Langley, was a regal white-haired elder statesman of a man, who had left his competent though somewhat imperious mark on the law firm that was one of the most respected in New York. His wife was tall, reed-slender, and endowed with a natural grace and elegance.

"Come with me, Samantha—" she threw a laughing look at Max "—and tell me about that lovely little girl of yours. It's ages since I saw her...she must be quite a little miss by now, and probably gorgeous. Of course, I've seen her pictures on Max's desk, but pictures never do anyone real justice, do they?"

Samantha gave Max a bemused look. It hadn't occurred to her, though perhaps it should have, that he would still be displaying pictures of Annie in his office. She remembered now that her own picture had once occupied a place of prominence on his desk, but that would have disappeared long ago. Max grinned back at her, an encouraging grin, one that seemed to say, "See, I told you it would be okay."

Samantha walked away with Nora, stopping here and there to acknowledge the greetings of other lawyers and their spouses. Their friendliness was so reassuring that she knew Max had been right when he'd said she would enjoy herself.

"We're all glad you're back." It was as much as the gracious Nora would ever allow herself to say about Samantha's lengthy absence. After that, she concentrated on asking about Annie.

"If it isn't Samantha Anderson," a familiar voice cut into the conversation. Turning, she found herself looking into the austere face of Stan Manson. He, too, seemed happy—and not at all surprised—to see her.

"I'm leaving you in good hands," Nora said, and moved away to welcome newly arriving guests.

For a few minutes Samantha stood talking to Stan. To her relief, he, too, made things easy for her. Without referring directly to William Anderson's will, he intimated that he was glad she had decided to do the right thing for her daughter. He knew more about Samantha than she had realized, for he then asked her about her job.

Samantha was just starting to tell him about the Tweedle brothers, when there was a call on his cellular phone. Excusing himself with a rueful smile, Stan moved away to take the call elsewhere, where he could speak without having to shout above the noise of the guests.

Left alone, Samantha spent a few minutes looking at the wonderful paintings that adorned the spacious room, before deciding to rejoin Max. He was easy to spot, even though he was on the other side of the room; well over six feet tall, he was by far the most impressive man at the party.

Samantha was no longer surprised at the sheer jolt of plea-sure she felt at the mere sight of him.

Engrossed in conversation, he didn't see her coming. Making her way through the crowd, Samantha was almost at his side, when she stopped abruptly. *Edna.* Her hand was on Max's arm, perfectly manicured fingers folded around the sleeve of his jacket. She was talking vivaciously, and he was laughing at something she said.

What on earth was Edna doing here? She wasn't a part-ner, and Max had said—implicitly—that Samantha would not run into her tonight. *How could he have lied to her?*

Samantha's first impulse was to walk away before they saw her, before she could be humiliated. But they would see her go, and laugh behind her back, and that would be much worse. Taking a breath, she lifted her head and straightened her shoulders.

"Hello, Edna."

Edna turned. She was a beautiful woman, as sensuous and exotic as Samantha remembered her. Her hair was jet-black and glossy, and her eyes were dark and striking. She was taller than Samantha, her figure slender and yet at the same time voluptuous. Her eyes had a come-hither look that many men could not resist—Max among them—but Samantha found her hard and unappealing

"Samantha." Her voice was cool and a little amused. "How nice you look."

"Thank you," Samantha responded lightly, making no attempt to return the blatantly insincere compliment.

Eyes sparkling with malice, Edna looked her up and down. Beside her, Max seemed a little tense. Samantha saw he was watching her enquiringly, as if he was not quite sure how she was going to react to the other woman. She looked back at him, her eyes meeting his directly. She was terribly angry, but since she knew her best tactic was not to show it, her emotion was reflected only in the hands that were clenched tightly at her sides.

"Samantha—" he began, but Edna interrupted him.

"Max—" the hand with the long red nails was still on his sleeve "—won't you get us something to drink? What will you have, Samantha? Diet soda?" A brittle laugh. "I'm sure they'll have that. Same as always for me, Max— gin and tonic, more gin than tonic."

The last words were spoken with a husky and deliberate intimacy. The fact was, Max seemed to know exactly what Edna wanted without hearing an exact description. Again, Samantha resolved not to give either of them the satisfaction of seeing her anger.

Edna's hand left Max's arm, but he waited a moment, as if wondering whether to leave Samantha alone with the woman she detested. Looking at her, he asked, "Is diet soda what you want?"

"Sure," she said brightly, when really she couldn't have cared less what he brought her. Actually she didn't want anything at all.

Max hesitated a moment longer, then moved away in the direction of the bar.

Now what? Samantha wondered. Should she walk away, too? Could she, without making a complete idiot of herself?

Once more, Edna took the lead. "So you're back. Should I say it's a surprise?"

"Why would you," Samantha said flatly, "when it obviously isn't?"

Edna laughed, a low and husky laugh, as sexy as everything else about her. "I won't in that case. How long exactly since the last time we saw each other?"

"Eleven months. Plus some days, if you want to be exact. Not that you need me to tell you, because I'm sure you remember."

Edna laughed again, setting Samantha's teeth on edge.

"Actually I haven't been counting." Dark eyes glittered with malice. "What I do remember is that you didn't say goodbye."

Stunned by her audacity, Samantha stared at Edna a moment before taking a quick step backward. She hadn't expected even Edna to be quite so outrageous.

"I think I'll look for Max," she muttered.

Edna gripped her arm before she could move away. "As much a ninny as ever, are you?" she mocked.

Samantha wrenched away. "What the hell do you mean?" she got out, over a dry throat.

"I'll never forget your expression when you found me in bed with your precious Max. You looked as if you were going to die on the spot. And the way you ran out of the room, as if you'd seen a devil and thought it was after you."

"A devil," Samantha agreed tightly. "With a female face. That's exactly what I saw."

The look Edna gave her was so hard and penetrating, that Samantha wondered if she had hit a raw spot.

But all Edna said was, "I'd have thought that after a few years of marriage you'd know how to deal with your husband. Men do stray, you know." That hateful laughter again. "So tell me, are you still as insecure as ever?"

Samantha lifted her head. "I'm not insecure at all. I don't have reason to be. But for your information, Edna, I've told Max not to bring you to the house while I'm there. I won't have you upsetting my daughter."

The strangest expression flashed across the exotic face, almost, Samantha thought, as if she had said something the other woman hadn't expected to hear. The expression didn't last—it was replaced by triumph. "And if I did come—what would you do? More to the point, what would you do if you found us in bed together again?"

Samantha thought she was going to be sick. Edna's outrageousness was far beyond anything she had ever encountered. How could Max be attracted to anyone so vicious? The answer was simple: Edna was sexy, and men were turned on by her.

"I don't owe you an answer," she said, when she could speak.

"Meaning the little mouse would run again," Edna said mockingly. "You haven't said—do you actually intend to stay with Max?"

Where was Max with their drinks? Samantha didn't know how much longer she could endure Edna's venom.

"That's why I'm here."

"Well, of course. You'll stay six months." Edna's expression was more malicious than ever. "Six months—no matter what it costs you. Sweet, innocent Samantha, even you have your price. Or at least you do for your daughter."

Samantha felt ill. "You know about my father-in-law's will?"

Edna was watching her closely. "I think that's obvious."

"Max told you?"

"I know—isn't that enough for you?" Edna turned her head. "Here he is now with the drinks. And not a moment too soon, Max. Your lovely wife looks as if she could do with something."

Max's eyes were narrow as he looked from one woman to the other. "I see you've been talking," he said, as he handed them each a glass. "Did I miss something?"

"Not a thing. Unless you happen to enjoy female chit-chat, and I know you don't." Edna shot him a flirtatious glance.

He glanced at her another moment, before turning again to Samantha. She saw the question in his expression, but she only looked back at him stonily. Then her gaze dropped to her glass, as she forced herself to take a sip.

Without a word to Max or Edna, Samantha moved away

from them. She began to circulate once more among the other guests, moving almost blindly through the room, hardly aware of the people who spoke to her, not concentrating on the things they said, hoping they would take the occasional nod as a sign of understanding. Not once did she glance backward. If Max and Edna were still absorbed in their own little world, she did not want to know about it. More than that, she wasn't going to give either of them the satisfaction of seeing that she was very close to tears.

Mercifully they left the party before most of the other guests. As they said goodbye to their hosts, Samantha allowed Max to hold her arm. The moment the door closed behind them, she jerked violently away from him.

They did not speak as Max started the car. It was only when they were driving that he said, "Want to tell me what happened?"

Furiously she turned on him. "I can't believe you're asking me that!"

His hands tightened on the wheel. "I *am* asking you. What happened, Samantha?"

"You didn't have the *decency* to tell me your mistress was going to be at the party. You knew I wouldn't have come if I'd known."

"Samantha—"

"You *lied* to me, Max! I asked you whether she was coming."

Taking his eyes off the road, Max turned to her briefly. "I was wrong. I'm sorry."

"A partners' party—isn't that what you told me? And Edna isn't a partner. Or so you said."

"She isn't. Yet. There's been talk lately of making her a partner, but she isn't one yet. I didn't know that Charles Langley decided to invite her." He turned to her again. "Do you believe me?"

It was a long time since Samantha had been quite so livid. "I don't!"

His lips tightened. "What possible reason could I have for lying to you?"

"You wanted me to meet your mistress. Wanted me to know that nothing had changed between you."

"At a party? It doesn't make sense, Samantha."

"To any sane person it wouldn't. But I'd asked you not to bring her to the house. I threatened to take Annie away with me if you did. Obviously it was so important for you to bring us together—heaven only knows why—that you chose another way."

"This is crazy, Samantha! I didn't know she'd be there tonight. I wish you'd believe me."

"I might, I just might, Max, if it wasn't for the things she said. Edna knows the terms of William's will." As he jerked, she added, "I guess I shouldn't be surprised you discussed it with her, though I hoped some things were off limits. I should have known better."

Max gripped the steering wheel with unusual force. It was a few seconds before he spoke again. "If I told you I didn't talk to Edna about the will, I guess you wouldn't believe that, either?"

"Damn right, I wouldn't!" Samantha exploded. "At this stage, there's not a single thing you could say I'd believe."

"In that case," Max said tightly, "there's no purpose in talking."

CHAPTER FIVE

WHEN Brian phoned the next day, Samantha was amazingly happy to hear his voice. It wasn't the first time he'd called since she had left Manhattan, but whenever he suggested getting together she said no. Max wouldn't take kindly to her seeing another man. A disgruntled Brian had had no option but to accept the situation.

"Brian!" she exclaimed.

"Well. For once, you actually sound pleased to hear my voice."

"It's good to know I still have a friend."

"More than a friend, I keep hoping." His voice had changed.

Samantha was silent a moment. She had spent several sleepless hours the previous night, brooding over what had happened at the party, furious at Edna, even more furious at Max. Some of her anger was even directed at herself, as she wondered if she should have guessed she was walking into a trap. But she had believed Max when he'd told her Edna wouldn't be there—perhaps because she had wanted so much to believe him.

And now here was Brian—at this moment he seemed her one friend in the world—and she had to be careful not to give him the wrong impression. If she did, she would be as guilty as Max.

"A friend," she said very gently, "but such a good friend, Brian."

"I'm crazy about you, Samantha! You know I want more than friendship."

"Brian... There can't be more, I've told you that."

"I won't press you." His voice changed again. "At least not now. Not until you leave that rotten so-called husband of yours. I mean, we both know you're not going to be with him more than six months."

Briefly Samantha closed her eyes, unprepared for the stab of pain the words brought her. She gripped the receiver tightly, knowing she had to make herself clear. "I won't be here long, but even after I leave, things won't change. You have to know that. Leaving Max won't make a difference to us. Brian, I'm sorry."

It was Brian's turn for silence. At length, he said, "I'm not ready to give up on you just yet."

"Brian..." She was beginning to wish he hadn't called after all.

He cut in before she could say more. "How are you and Annie?"

"Fine. Just fine."

"Why don't I believe you?"

"We really are fine," Samantha said quickly.

"I don't think you're telling the truth. Max treating you badly?"

"Nothing like that!"

"Something's wrong, I can tell by your voice. What is it, Samantha?"

"Nothing I want to talk about. Anyway, I'm probably just feeling sorry for myself."

"I can do something about that." Brian was suddenly animated. "It's Saturday, and you're not working, are you? Why don't we go to the zoo, you and me and Annie?"

Samantha took her time about answering. She glanced across the room at Annie, who was absorbed in a jigsaw puzzle. In the hallway, Helen was vacuuming; all the chores were taken care of, so that there was nothing for Samantha to do.

As for Max, he must have left the house very early, for

he was gone by the time Samantha and Annie had come downstairs to breakfast. Samantha knew he was busy working on a case that was coming up shortly, and when that happened he often spent weekends in the office, glad of the chance to get some concentrated work done when the phones were quiet and there was nobody around to disturb him.

There was also the possibility that he'd gone to see Edna. If that was the case, were the two of them laughing at the events of last night? Worse still, were they making love? The thought made her feel ill.

"Samantha—are you still there?"

"Yes…"

"Will you come with me? Or are you scared your lord and master won't give you permission?"

Lord and master, indeed. And as for permission! The words did it. Brian seemed to think Max could order her around and expect obedience.

"Nobody tells me what I can do," she said tightly. "I'm my own person. Always."

Brian chuckled. "Max must have done something really terrible to get you worked up like this. Ordinarily you're so easygoing."

Max had done the unforgivable, but Brian didn't have to know the details. "The zoo?" she asked abruptly. "When were you thinking of going?"

"You'll come? Whoopee! Let's see… I can be there in an hour or so—that suit you?"

An hour. Would Max be back by then? Unlikely. Besides, she didn't owe it to her precious husband—her rotten so-called husband, as Brian had called him—to be at home when he returned. She owed Max nothing, she told herself again grimly.

Brian arrived an hour later, and was visibly impressed as he took in his surroundings. "Quite some place!" he exclaimed, and Samantha, trying to see the house through his eyes, thought she detected a note of envy in his tone. Yet as they drove away, he was once more his usual cheerful self. Only once did he allude to Max's apparent wealth, but when Samantha pointed out that money did not influence her attitude toward people, he was quick to change the subject.

Annie loved the zoo. No matter how often she went, she was always as excited as if she was seeing the animals for the first time. She had her firm favorites: the elephants, swishing the ground with their long trunks; the peacocks, especially the males with their jeweled plumage; and the tigers, which awed and intimidated her. More than anything, she loved the monkeys.

It was difficult to distract her once they reached the monkey cage. As the monkeys swung from branches, played and squabbled, Annie's laughter was joyful and unrestrained.

"I've missed her," Brian said. "I've missed you both. More than you realize."

As his arm went around Samantha's shoulder, her initial reaction was shock of a kind. It wasn't the first time Brian had touched her; he had even kissed her on occasion, and she hadn't minded. But this was different. For some reason—one that involved Max—it seemed wrong.

Without meaning to, she flinched. Beside her, Brian stiffened.

"You're not going to call that a lewd pass?"

Samantha forced herself to ignore the sullen tone. "Of course not, and I'm sorry."

"Friends do touch, Samantha. It's not as if I'm trying to have sex with you."

"I know that," she said, as calmly as she could. Brian had done her a favor by taking her away from the house for a few hours. It wasn't his fault that she was so on edge today. She made herself smile at him. "I did say I was sorry."

But he couldn't leave it at that. "It's Max, isn't it?"

"Brian..."

"Still in love with him, Samantha?"

Brian's arm tightened around her shoulder as he asked the question. Samantha, repelled, wanted to move away, but she forced herself to stand still.

"Are you?" he persisted.

She looked up at him, and was dismayed to see that eyes, which had always been clear and cheerful, were annoyed now. "Max is my husband," she said carefully.

The hold on her shoulder intensified further. "I wouldn't say that."

"We're not divorced."

"You will be soon." Brian paused a moment. "You haven't changed your mind, have you?"

Even if she had, it would make no difference. Last night had been proof of that. Whatever her feelings for Max— and Samantha knew now that her feelings were all too real—Max's feelings were reserved for Edna.

"If you're asking whether we'll stay together—I doubt it."

Leave it at that, she begged him wordlessly. For a few minutes they stood silently together, pretending to watch Annie making funny faces at the monkeys, when in reality their thoughts were on themselves.

Samantha was acutely aware of the arm holding her: an awareness that was altogether different from anything she'd ever felt with Max. With Max, all contact was vibrant, sexual even when they were not actually touching. Samantha couldn't be in a confined space with Max, a room or a car, without the sense that the air around them was charged. Even when she was angry with him, desire was never far from the surface. He excited her in a way no other man had ever had the power to do.

Brian's body so close to hers was lifeless, sexless, with no power to stir her. With all her heart, Samantha wished things could be different, for she sensed that she might never be able to respond physically to any man but Max. Yet the fact was that she couldn't force herself to feel something that wasn't there.

"Do you sleep with him?"

Samantha's head jerked. "I can't believe you asked that!"

"Well, do you?" Despite her reaction, Brian didn't look in the least apologetic. "Hell, Samantha, the man has a mistress. Don't look at me like that—after all, you were the one who caught him in bed with the woman."

Samantha was outraged. "You're way out of line!"

"Then you have been sleeping with him. You do. Which explains the way you're reacting to me." His face was flushed, his eyes stormy.

Samantha took a few steps away from him. "As it happens, I haven't been sleeping with Max. But if I had, it wouldn't concern you."

Her anger must have got through to Brian, for he looked uncertain all at once. "I'm sorry... I didn't mean to... It's just that I get so mad when I think of you with that man." He looked at her pleadingly. "You do understand, don't you, Samantha?"

"I understand it was a mistake to come with you today." Her anger had faded somewhat.

"No," he insisted.

"Yes," she said gently. "It isn't your fault, Brian. I know you meant well, and you haven't done anything wrong. If anything, you tried to give us some happiness."

"Well then, there you are." There was a hint of truculence in his tone.

"All the same, I shouldn't have come. Not while I'm living with Max, while there's so much to sort out in my mind."

"Samantha... What are you trying to tell me?"

"That we can't get together again. I'm sorry, Brian, but it really was a mistake. My mistake. Only mine."

Still captivated by the monkeys, Annie hadn't heard a word the adults were saying, and was unaware of their tension. When her mother called her name, she didn't respond. It was only when Samantha touched her arm that she turned.

"Time to go, honey."

The little girl's face fell. "Can't we stay longer, Mommy?"

"No, Annie, we really do have to go now."

The child looked at Brian, as if she hoped he would encourage her mother to change her mind. But the man only looked at her sadly, and shook his head.

On the way home, Samantha stared guiltily out of the window. She shouldn't have accepted Brian's invitation, she realized. She had acted out of anger, and in the end she hadn't been fair to Brian. Without meaning to, she had tried to make him a substitute for Max.

If the disastrous morning had achieved anything, it was that she had acquired a degree of self-knowledge. She had learned that spending time with another man accomplished absolutely nothing. All it did was highlight the fact that she was in love with her husband. And much good that did her, she thought wryly.

A grim-faced man awaited them as they got out of Brian's car.

"The guy is angry," Brian said in an undertone.

That was putting it mildly. "What you get up to with

Samantha in New York is none of my business," Max told Brian, his words clipped, his eyes cold as steel, "but I expect you to stay away from my wife while she's living in my house."

Samantha held her breath as she saw Brian bristle. His hands clenched into fists and his shoulders squared, so that for a few seconds he looked like a dog about to go on the attack. Max was not a man who settled issues with fisticuffs, but in his university days he had been a superb boxer. Even now, he was all hard muscle. His superior height and strength gave him the advantage any time over the smaller, softer man.

"Go," Samantha advised Brian quietly.

Brian shot Max a venomous look. "Take care of her—or you'll have me to reckon with."

But he didn't press the issue further than that. After hugging Annie, he said goodbye to Samantha, got back in the car and drove away.

"Daddy!" Annie jumped into her father's arms. "We went to the zoo, and we had such fun. You should have seen the monkeys, Daddy. Why didn't you come with us?"

Max kissed the top of her head. "Perhaps we'll have a good time ourselves tomorrow, princess." He put her down. "Why don't you run along to the kitchen? Helen just took some cookies out of the oven, and she told me she made them especially for you."

Annie ran off, and Samantha was about to follow her into the house, when Max said her name.

She turned. "Yes?"

"We have to talk." He was stony-faced.

"Now? It's been a long morning."

"Right now. This outing with your boyfriend. What was it all about?"

It was on the tip of Samantha's tongue to tell Max that

Brian was not her boyfriend and never had been, but at the last minute something kept her back. His anger gave her enormous satisfaction. If Max was shocked, it was no more than he deserved. Certainly he hadn't earned a right to the truth.

Pleasantly she said, "Brian invited us to the zoo, I accepted."

"How dare you?"

"Don't go making a big deal of nothing, Max."

"Nothing?" His voice was like ice, a dangerous tone, Samantha recognized with a small shiver of excitement and apprehension. "You came back here as my wife. I leave the house for a few hours, and I get back to find you gone with that man. You and my daughter."

Samantha was glad Annie was out of earshot. It wouldn't do for the little girl to hear her parents' angry words.

"You have some nerve, Max!" she exclaimed heatedly. "You go to bed with Edna, and that's okay. I spend some innocent time at the zoo with Brian and Annie, and I've committed a major crime. Double standards, Max. Or didn't you know that?"

"You don't know what the hell you're talking about!" he said harshly.

"Wrong!" She threw the word at him. "I do know what I'm saying. What I do in my spare time is my own business. It doesn't concern you, hasn't since the day you decided to start an affair."

They stood glaring at each other, faces pale with emotion, breathing rapid. Samantha saw that Max was stressed. In normal circumstances, she would have been sympathetic. But she was stressed, too, had been since last night, and she wasn't going to waste her energy on Max.

She was about to walk off again, when he caught her arm. "We haven't finished."

Furiously she jerked away from him. "Maybe you haven't. My head is splitting, and I'm going inside."

When Max was angry, his eyes were hard and dark as polished onyx. "I won't have you seeing that man again. Not while you're living in this house. Nor will I have him spending any time with my daughter. Understand?"

At that moment, Samantha felt as if she never wanted to see either of the men again. Max and Brian, both of them more trouble than they were worth. Although to be fair, Brian had never done her any harm: Max was the one who had caused her a year of anguish.

"My daughter, too, for the record," she said crisply. "And don't give me orders, Max. William's will only stipulated that Annie and I had to spend six months here. Correct me if I'm wrong, but I'm willing to bet there were no conditions attached to my social life. If I want to see Brian—or any other man—I'll do so. *Without* your permission, Max."

Brave words, she reflected wryly, yet meaningless, because all she was doing was making a statement. After the fiasco at the zoo, she knew she wouldn't be seeing other men while she was still Max's wife.

She was almost at the house when Max caught up with her again. "Samantha."

She put a hand to her throbbing head. "Now what? Can't you see I've had enough for now?"

"Your head really hurts?" He touched her forehead, quite gently, but Samantha couldn't tell whether the gesture was genuinely solicitous or merely pretence. "Poor Samantha."

Though his voice was softer now, she thought he was probably being sarcastic. "Spare me the sympathy, Max. I just need to get to my room."

"In a moment. Whatever you may think, I was not with Edna this morning."

She looked at him warily. "After last night—how can I believe you?"

"It's true. I've been busy with a case, and that's why I went to the office." Dark eyes were steady and clear, and his tone had a ring of truth.

"Want to know why I came back early, Samantha?"

"Not particularly."

"I'll tell you anyway. I had an outing planned. Thought we'd go to the beach. You and me and Annie. Imagine how I felt when I found you weren't here."

Head throbbing, Samantha looked at him, this man whose mood seemed to change so quickly from one minute to the next: the man she had once thought she knew so well, and found she didn't know at all.

"I was disappointed," he told her. "But that's water under the bridge now. We'll go tomorrow instead. Annie will love it."

"You can go with Annie, Max. I've absolutely no interest in going to the beach with you."

Max pushed some hair from her forehead in a gesture that felt like a caress. Samantha swallowed hard on the lump that formed in her throat.

"Go to your room," he said softly. "I'll bring you a cup of tea and something for the pain."

Taken aback, she could only murmur, "Thank you."

Her hand was on the back door of the house, when Max said, "You may want to change your mind about tomorrow." Putting a finger on her lips, he silenced her refusal. "Don't say anything now. When you've had time to sleep on it, you can tell me what you've decided."

"Glad you came?"

Samantha turned her eyes from the volleyball game she

had been watching, and looked instead at the superb male figure at her side. Indeed, it had been to stop herself from focusing on Max that she had concentrated her attention on the game in the first place. Six foot three of lithe, tanned limbs and hard muscles, he was the most spectacular man on the beach.

"Yes," she said shortly, understanding that Max would know she was lying if she said anything else.

Last night, furious as she had been with him, she had made up her mind to skip the outing. By this morning, however, her fighting spirit had weakened. The blue sky with its promise of a perfect day; the animated little girl, hardly able to contain her excitement at the thought of going to the beach; and the vibrantly handsome man, who renewed his invitation with sparkling eyes and a daredevil grin: all these had combined to make it impossible for a normal woman to resist.

"Meaning you've decided to believe me when I tell you I didn't know Edna would be at the party? And that I wasn't with her yesterday?"

"Meaning I've put Edna out of my mind for today." She shot him a mischievous grin, aware that she was purposely evading the question. "Might as well enjoy myself now that I'm here."

Max's lips tightened—clearly the answer was not the one he had wanted. He seemed about to say something, but at that moment Annie turned and said, "What are you talking about?"

Her father pushed a playful hand through her curls. "Adult talk, princess. Shall we make a sand castle? And in the meanwhile your mommy—" a meaningful look at Samantha "—may want to go and get into something a little less overdressed?"

"I'm perfectly comfortable," Samantha protested, looking down at her shirt and jeans.

"You used to be a bikini-girl."

Samantha had always loved the freedom of the beach, and still did. It was only the thought of having Max see her nearly naked after so long that had kept her in her street clothes until now. The wicked twinkle in his eyes told her that he'd read her thoughts exactly. She wondered if he knew that despite Edna, there was a part of her that yearned to be sexy in his eyes—so much so that at the last moment, and against her better judgment, she had shoved her bikini into the bottom of her beach bag.

She stood up. "I do want to swim." Avoiding Max's eyes, she smiled down at Annie. "Let's see if you can make a start on that sand castle before I get back."

Ten minutes later, Max saw his wife coming toward him again, and his heart skipped a few beats. After several years of motherhood, she was still the beautiful, utterly sexy and desirable girl who had captured his heart the first moment he had seen her. Graceful as a ballerina, she walked over the hard wet sand, a scarlet bikini showing off her lovely figure to perfection. There were the delectable breasts that he had once delighted in kissing, and the tiny waist, which even now would fit easily between his two hands. Her legs were smooth and shapely, and as he remembered the feel of them against his in their bed, he ached to caress them.

As she came closer he saw her eyes, big and green and surprisingly shy, as if she wondered how he would react to her. What would she say, he wondered, if he told her that there wasn't an hour in the day when he didn't hunger to make love to her? Probably, he thought, she would make some sarcastic comment about Edna.

Shifting her eyes from his, Samantha knelt down on the sand and admired the sand castle, which had started to take shape in her absence. On her way back, she had picked up some shells and a few bits of seaweed. For decoration, she said.

For a while, the three of them built the sand castle together, laughing and talking as they worked, and it occurred to Samantha that to any stranger they would look like a normal, happy family enjoying a day on the beach. The thought brought with it a great longing: if only they really were what they seemed, what they had once been.

Inevitably she and Max touched now and then, their hands meeting on the sand, their legs brushing against each other. Each time, Samantha experienced a familiar shiver of excitement. But more than sexual arousal, there was a *rightness* about the proximity with Max, whereas everything about the outing with Brian had been so very wrong.

When they had decorated the sand castle, Max said, "Time to make a tunnel."

"A tunnel?" Annie asked eagerly. "How, Daddy?"

"This is grown-up stuff, princess. You'll have to let Mommy and me do it. We have longer arms."

They began to burrow through the sand castle, Max on one side, Samantha on the other. As the tunnel lengthened, Samantha's anticipation grew. The moment came when their fingers met in the middle. Samantha didn't withdraw her hand as quickly as she could have—or perhaps she didn't want to—and in an instant, a strong finger hooked around one of hers. Holding fast, it reached for her hand and caressed the palm.

"Max..." Samantha's breathing quickened.

"Yes?" Dark eyes teased her.

"Tunnel's finished."

"Really?"

No man had the right to be quite so dynamic, she thought. But she only said, "Sure of it," and wished the words could have come out less jerkily.

Max released her finger, and the three of them put the finishing touches to their masterpiece. By now, Annie was beginning to grow a bit restless. A family with a little girl had settled themselves nearby, and Annie was excited when she recognized Linda, one of the children from her kindergarten group. Leaving the sand castle, she ran off to play with her friend.

"Quite a palace!" called Linda's mother.

Samantha had met the woman a few times. In no time, the four adults got into conversation, and Linda's parents were happy to oblige when Max asked whether they would watch Annie while he and Samantha went for a swim.

Samantha laughed when Max splashed her face with water, and lost no time in splashing him back. To Max, her joyful laughter was the most beautiful sound in the world. He thought she had never looked lovelier than with her eyes sparkling in the sunlight, and her wet face flushed with pleasure.

Samantha gasped when Max moved suddenly behind her, dived down into the water, pushed his head between her legs and stood up, lifting her with him. Sitting astride his shoulders, she laughed again, feeling as young and as carefree as a young girl frolicking with a special boyfriend. She buried her hands in Max's thick wet hair, reveling in the feel of it between her fingers, and wondering if he knew she was holding his hair not so much for security as for the sheer sensuous pleasure it gave her.

The laughter died in her throat when Max reached for her hands, lifting them out of his hair, and then pulling her forward over his head, until her mouth was just inches from his. His head was hard against her near-bare breasts now, and as he spoke her name, it seemed to pour from his lips right into her mouth. A moment later, he was pulling her still closer, until they were kissing.

Samantha had never experienced anything quite like this. The feel of Max's strong throat pressed hard between her thighs and against the secret, most vulnerable core of her being; his head against her breasts and throat; the sensuous and exploratory kisses. Her excitement was increasing by the second.

She could not have said later how long they remained in an embrace that was like nothing they had ever attempted before. When she thought about it, she knew only that time had stood still, and that if there were other people in the ocean, they had ceased to exist. There was only Max, her beloved Max, and the utterly incredible sensations he was arousing in her.

Max lowered her from his shoulders at length, but he didn't let go of her. Holding her close against him, he kissed the top of her hair, while his hands moved over her throat and down her back to her hips. She was so close to him now that she could feel the evidence of his own arousal against her, and that only made her even more excited.

"I want to make love to you." His lips moved against her ear as he spoke.

"Oh God, Max...." Her legs were so weak that if he hadn't been holding her so tightly they might have buckled.

"Let's go home, Samantha." His voice was rough.

She wanted to, just as much as he did. Even more, perhaps, because she had dreamed of it so often. Faintly she said, "Annie..."

"Helen will take care of her."

Hand in hand, they waded out of the water. Samantha's throat was dry with longing, her whole body was on fire. *This* was what she had been wanting for so long—to make love with Max. To spend hours in his arms.

"We'll get Annie's things together," Max said, as they were walking back up the beach.

"Yes!" Seconds later, she stood still. "No..."

Max stopped, too, and looked at her. "What's wrong?"

"It's no good." Her voice shook.

"What are you talking about?"

"We can't do it, Max."

"Why not?"

The gaze on her face was intent. If only he wasn't making her spell it out, especially now, when it was difficult for her just to say a few words.

"If you have something to say, say it." His eyes had narrowed.

"We can't do it."

"You want to as much as I do, Samantha."

She couldn't deny it—Max knew her too well, he would know she was lying. He had always known when she was in the mood for love, for her body gave her away every time. Scantily clothed as she was now, her nipples hard against the clinging wet fabric of her bikini, Max had only to look at her to be in no doubt as to her emotions. All the same, she had to resist him.

"It's no good," she said again. "Too much has changed."

"You keep saying that," Max said harshly. "Sometimes I think you use that phrase as a sort of generic excuse. No matter what you say, we're still married, still husband and wife."

"Husband and wife on the brink of divorce. That's the thing you seem to forget."

"A divorce that's going nowhere right now. That isn't written in stone, Samantha."

"Maybe not as far as you're concerned," she said unsteadily. "But then you seem to think you can have a wife as well as a mistress."

"I've never said that."

"You haven't had to. The fact is, you have your stan-

dards, and I have mine. And they don't happen to coin-
cide.''

Max was quiet for a long moment. Samantha forced herself to stand motionless as his gaze moved over her. It
lingered for a long time on eyes that were still smoky with
desire, and on the mouth that had joined his in erotic kisses,
before going quite blatantly to her breasts in their flimsy
scarlet covering.

"I don't think you believe a word you're saying,
Samantha, but I didn't bring you here to fight.''

"And I didn't come to be seduced.''

"Do you think that's why I planned this outing?'' he
demanded.

Samantha stood still, looking at Max without answering.
The sand was hot beneath her feet, and droplets of water
trailed from her wet hair onto her face. "I don't know what
to think any longer,'' she said at last, honestly.

"Making love might give you the answers you're looking for. Why not give it a try?''

"Everything begins and ends in bed for you, Max. That's
your starting point, isn't it? It's not as simple for me.''

Max gave a harsh laugh as his eyes ravaged her again,
even more blatantly this time. "You could have fooled
me.''

Samantha felt herself turn a deep red, but she managed
to stand her ground. "I'm not denying you turned me on,
Max. And all things being equal, you're right, I would want
to make love. But I can't forget Edna—in bed a year ago,
and at the party the other night.''

"I thought you'd put her out of your mind for today,''
Max said quietly.

"I did—for a while. Until a few minutes ago, and then
I realized I was being a fool. There are facts that don't go
away, no matter how hard you try to forget them.''

Max's lips tightened. "Can't you ever stop thinking about Edna? I wasn't talking about making love to her. It's you I want to take to bed. And you know it would be wonderful."

"Maybe it would." Samantha's voice shook. "But I'd only hate myself afterward, and I'm not prepared to let myself in for that kind of pain ever again."

For a moment she thought Max was about to say something, but he must have thought better of it, because his lips closed again very firmly.

They walked on, collected Annie and offered to look after Linda while her parents swam. But the offer was turned down: Linda's mother didn't feel like swimming that day, she said.

They stayed on the beach a while longer, taking Annie into the water to paddle. But the joy had gone out of the day, and eventually they decided to pack up and go home. They were turning into the driveway, when Max said, "Did I tell you Melissa is coming to visit?"

Samantha jerked. "Your sister?"

"I don't know any other Melissa," he said blandly.

"When?"

"Tomorrow."

"*Tomorrow?* Why didn't you mention it before now?"

"Must have slipped my mind. She called just as we were leaving."

Samantha stared at Max, aghast. "You could have said something. Where will she sleep?"

"Where does she usually sleep?"

"In the guest room. But you're in there now... What on earth will we do, Max?"

"I'll leave you to sort that one out." As he got out of the car, Max threw her a particularly jaunty look.

CHAPTER SIX

WHEN Samantha woke up the next morning, she spent at least half a minute enjoying the sunshine streaming in through the window. It was a few seconds before she remembered Melissa. When she did, she sat up with a start.

Max's sister, three years older than he was, had taken it upon herself to care for him after the death of their mother when they were both still very young. This was one of those cases where it was true that old habits die hard. There was a part of Melissa that had never accepted the fact that her brother was a competent lawyer, an adult well able to make his own decisions—even in his choice of a marriage partner.

It appeared that Melissa had already chosen a "suitable girl" for Max—someone who was thrilled at the thought of linking up with the very eligible Max Anderson, and appropriately eager to do whatever Melissa asked. When Max told his sister that he had already met the woman he was going to marry, she was upset. However, instead of letting out her anger on Max, she vented it on Samantha.

Samantha sometimes thought she would never be able to do anything right in Melissa's eyes. Ignore her, Max advised, but that was more easily said than done, particularly when it came to matters concerning the house. While Max and his father had lived there alone, backing it so to speak, they had been content to let Melissa make all the household decisions. Even Helen, though given to the occasional private grumble, did her bidding.

All this changed as Samantha's confidence increased, and her wishes as the new mistress of the house conflicted with an outraged Melissa's. Inevitably the two sisters-in-law were thrown together on Christmas and Thanksgiving, as well as all the birthdays. Samantha tried very hard to make these occasions as pleasant as possible, making sure that Melissa's favorite foods were always included in the menu, and trying to treat her as if she were a friend. But however hard she tried, Melissa was always somewhat hostile, so that Samantha couldn't help being tense before and during one of her visits.

And now Melissa was about to descend on them. On her. Samantha's head throbbed at the thought of what the next days might bring. That they would bring something, she was fairly certain. Where would her sister-in-law sleep? More to the point—*why was she coming?*

She could only guess at the answer to the second question, but with a bit of ingenuity, at least the first one could be solved. Melissa would have the guest room as usual. As for Max, he could move into the den—thank heavens for the studio couch—for the duration of his sister's visit.

She had just finished moving the last of Max's clothes into the den when she heard a car coming up the driveway. Looking out of the window, she saw Melissa getting out of a shiny new Buick. A quick look around the room to make sure everything was in order—all Max's belongings removed, a vase of fresh flowers and a few new magazines on the table by the bed—then she ran down the stairs, and was at the door when the bell gave an imperious ring.

"Hi," she said, with a smile. "It's been a while, Melissa."

"Hello, Samantha." Melissa's answering smile was so frosty that Samantha's heart sank.

"Come inside," she said, as cheerfully as she could.

"I hardly think I need an invitation."

Determined to keep the visit as cordial as possible,

Samantha bit back the retort that leaped instinctively to her lips. "Of course you don't."

The last time she had seen her sister-in-law had been at William's funeral. Melissa had adored her father, and his death had hit her hard. Melissa was divorced, and having no sister or other close female relative, she had allowed Samantha to comfort her. Now she seemed to have reverted to her usual combativeness.

It was a lovely day, and Samantha suggested they go and sit on the patio. Annie came running out. When she saw her aunt, she hung back for a moment, but Melissa held out her arms, and she submitted to a hug.

"Looks very thin." Melissa mouthed the words over the child's head.

"She's fine," Samantha answered quietly.

"Is she eating?"

Samantha suppressed a sigh at one of the familiar bones of contention between Melissa and herself. "Yes."

She was glad when Helen arrived with a tray of coffee and sandwiches. Melissa told the housekeeper that the brass handle of the front door needed polishing, but her manner lacked its usual vigor. It was obvious she had something on her mind. They couldn't talk in front of Annie, and the sooner Melissa said what she had to, the better for all of them. Samantha made a small signal to Helen, who took the little girl with her into the house.

"So you're back," said Max's sister, when Samantha had poured the coffee and offered her a sandwich.

"Right." Wondering whether she only imagined an accusation in her sister-in-law's tone, Samantha decided to be assertive. "But you knew that, didn't you?"

"Yes. Though if you think Max told me, you're wrong." A bitter expression crossed Melissa's face. "My brother has been secretive since the day he met you."

Samantha took a sip of coffee, even though she didn't

really feel like it: she had to give herself a second or two to control her anger. "And you blame me for that?" she asked at last.

"No use pretending I don't. I never did think you were the right person for Max, but of course he thought he knew better. Well, at least that situation is about to end."

Samantha was holding the delicate cup so tightly that she thought it might break. Putting it down, she said, "Max told you that?"

Melissa threw her a contemptuous look. "He didn't have to. I'm not an idiot. You've been away almost a year. It's not difficult to draw conclusions."

"I'm back now."

"For six months."

This was almost like a replay of the conversation with Edna. It was becoming increasingly difficult for Samantha to keep her anger at bay. "So you and Max *have* been talking about me."

"Actually he's refused to answer my questions."

A fierce joy surged through Samantha as she stared at Melissa. Had Max been more loyal than she'd realized?

"He didn't have to say anything," Melissa went on, "though it would've been nice if he'd taken me into his confidence. I know you're back for six months." She looked at Samantha contemptuously. "I've read Dad's will many times—I'm a beneficiary, too, remember?"

Foolish of her not to have thought that. "So you know the condition your father made with regard to Annie's inheritance?"

Melissa knew, Edna knew. Who else knew why she had gone back to Max? And were they all viewing her with that same hateful contempt?

"Sure, I know the conditions. Can't imagine what made him do it."

"Apparently," Samantha said quietly, "your father was hoping Max and I would get together again."

"I could have told him it wouldn't happen. If he'd really wanted to leave Annie an inheritance, he should have just gone ahead and done it. Doesn't make sense for him to attach strings."

Ironic that Melissa, of all people, should be echoing Samantha's thoughts. Ironic, too, that Samantha felt driven to defend her beloved father-in-law's well-meant but misguided intentions. "He must have had his reasons."

"Of course. He thought the world of you. He fell for your prettiness and high spirits, just as Max did. He never did catch on to the fact it was all just skin-deep. God, men are such fools."

Max's sister was jealous of her! And for some reason, Samantha had never realized it.

"Melissa…" she began gently, reaching out to touch her sister-in-law's hand. "Melissa, I never—" She stopped as the other woman snatched back her hand.

"Dad was devastated when you left the house. Kept hoping you'd be back. Max wouldn't talk, wouldn't say what happened. Not that he had to."

"What do you mean?" Samantha whispered, appalled. Melissa had never made a secret of her dislike, but she had never before been quite so openly hostile.

"Well, it was obvious, wasn't it? You married Max thinking he'd give you a life of luxury, and you were right about that. I guess you also thought he'd be dancing attendance on you every moment of the day. Must have been a shock when you realized that he had a life apart from you, one you couldn't share. A life spent in court, and with other lawyers…people on the same wavelength as him."

Edna, Samantha thought. Was she talking about Edna? Or had Max kept his mistress a secret from both his father and his sister? She was beginning to think this might be the case.

"But in the end, you were bored. In a way I can sympathize with you, Samantha, because I've been through something similar myself. Stuck with a man who could never descend to your intellectual level. Who could only love you for your appearance. And so you just up and went, depriving Dad of the granddaughter he adored. As for my brother, all he's had are the occasional visits with Annie."

Samantha couldn't believe what she was hearing. "You don't know anything about it!"

"Don't I? At least, I know why you came back. You want your daughter to have her money. As for putting your marriage together again, Dad was crazy if he thought it could work. I know you, Samantha, you'll be out of here the day the six months are up. I'm willing to bet you and Max aren't even sharing a room, much less a bed."

"Our sleeping arrangements are none of your business," Samantha countered hotly.

"Wrong. Max isn't the only executor of Dad's estate."

"There's Stan Manson..."

"That's right. If I tell Stan that you and Max aren't making a real attempt to get together again—that you're both just putting on an act—Annie's inheritance will be history."

"In other words," Samantha said slowly, "you've come here to spy."

"Call it whatever you like."

Samantha looked curiously at the woman who was in some ways so much like her brother. Without the bitterness etching her face, she could have been beautiful. "Why are you doing this, Melissa?"

"It's simple—I'm doing this for my father." Melissa's eyes were bleak. "I loved him, and I hate to see the two of you making a fool of him now that he's gone. Does that answer your question, Samantha?''

Strangely it did. Whatever Melissa's faults, her loyalty to her father was beyond question. Samantha believed her when she said she had come to make sure her father's wishes were being respected.

To say that Max was amazed when he found his belongings back in the master bedroom—Samantha had moved them from the den while Melissa was taking a shower—would have been an understatement.

"I had no idea you were going to spring this on me!" he exclaimed.

"Don't make too much of it," she said dryly.

He came to her and put his arms around her, and for a moment she allowed herself the luxury of leaning her head against his chest. Against her cheek, she could feel the hard beat of his heart, and the male smell of him was familiarly intoxicating. With her eyes closed, Samantha could pretend they were really together again, husband and wife, in their bedroom, where later that night they would make love.

Presently he spoke into her ear. "After yesterday, I hoped this would happen."

Dazed by his closeness and the effect he was having on her, she wasn't thinking clearly. "Yesterday...?"

"In the ocean. I sensed your excitement when we were kissing."

Samantha stepped out of his arms. "It's nothing like that."

But Max went on, as if he hadn't heard her. "I told you I wanted to make love. You wanted it too, darling. I could feel it."

He was reaching for her again. Inside Samantha, desire was stirring, flaming to life with all the intensity of a brush-fire. She wanted nothing more than to make love with Max, but the small sane voice at the edge of her mind told her it was important to make things clear to him quickly, before the situation spiraled out of control.

"No…" Reluctantly she took another step backward.

"What's wrong, darling? Are you thinking about Annie?" Clearly Max had misunderstood. "Can Helen look after her?"

"Max—it isn't just Annie. Melissa is here."

"Shoot, I forgot she was coming!" He struck his head in frustration. "Had a heck of a day, and Melissa's visit went right out of my mind." Max reached for Samantha again, looking puzzled when she moved out of his way. "Guess we'll have to postpone making love until later tonight." His voice roughened. "I don't know if I can wait, Samantha. It's been so long."

"This isn't what you think," she said flatly. "I had to put Melissa in the guest room. *That's* why you're in here. The only reason, Max."

The joy left Max's face. His breathing was still a little ragged, but he managed to say, "You didn't think of the den? Would have been a lot easier on our hormones than this."

"I did think of it," she acknowledged, "but Melissa is here to spy on us."

"Give me a break, Samantha!"

"No, really. She doesn't believe we're honestly trying to make another go of our marriage."

"Are we?" he drawled.

"No," Samantha said after a moment.

"Ever feel guilty that we haven't done more?"

"Guilty? Not exactly. Six months in this house, the will said. Nothing about sharing a room…making love…"

"But you do know what Dad wanted."

"I think I know what he *hoped*. And I feel bad about it, because I loved him."

"It's not too late to begin."

"But it is too late, Max," she said fiercely. "There's still Edna."

"Always Edna. Samantha, don't you think it's time you let me—"

"*No!*" She threw the word at him fiercely. "I *won't* talk about her. I can't, and you know it! You talk about your dad's will, and the hopes he had for us. I was in a trap, Max, virtually forced to come back here for Annie's sake—when I never wanted to have anything to do with you again. And now Melissa is here. After all we've gone through, we can't have her telling tales to Stan Manson. That's why I moved your things back into this room, Max."

Max's eyes went over her in that way he had, making her yearn to forget everything she had just said. When he spoke at last, his voice was soft, husky and infinitely seductive. "Are you telling me that sleeping together in one bed will do nothing for your libido?"

In an instant, she was trembling. "Who said anything about one bed?" Her voice shook.

Max laughed softly. "There's only one in this room."

"You don't have to sleep in it," Samantha said, a little wildly.

"Where did you think I'd sleep?"

She was unable to look at him, knowing that the expression in her eyes would betray her. "We could put a few chairs together."

Max laughed again. "Oh, no, my darling wife. If I'm going to be in this room, we'll sleep in the same bed. And let the consequences take care of themselves."

It was just as well that Max and Melissa hadn't seen each other for some time, and had lots to talk about. Samantha was silent through most of the meal. Had she been asked, she wouldn't have remembered a single topic of conversation.

She tried to keep her thoughts away from the bedroom with its enticing double bed, but the pictures that formed behind her eyes appeared there involuntarily, and were impossible to push away. Her emotions were a mixture of excitement and desire, but there was also the anger that came whenever she thought of Max's betrayal. She tried to hold on to the anger, but the other emotions seemed to be gaining the upper hand, at least for now.

Occasionally Max or Melissa would turn to her, as if to include her in the conversation, and she would make some noncommittal remark, which she could only hope would be taken for intelligent response. Fortunately, brother and sister were so busy catching up on news of family and friends that not much was demanded of Samantha.

She jerked when she heard her name. It came to her that Max had been addressing her, and not for the first time.

"Yes?"

"I was saying it was time for bed."

Samantha tensed as she saw two pairs of eyes, both so alike, watching her intently. Forcing an expression of calm, she murmured, "It's that late? I hadn't realized."

"Hadn't you, darling?" Max asked.

Before Samantha could answer, Melissa said, "You've seemed distracted all evening. I wondered why."

Involuntarily Samantha glanced at Max. The eye furthest from Melissa closed in a deliberate wink, so blatant that Samantha was unable to prevent the flush that instantly heated her cheeks. She couldn't even allow herself an angry look back at him, because that would betray them both.

As casually as she could, she said, "Sorry, I had a few things on my mind."

"Care to tell us about them?" Max drawled. "Melissa

and I have been monopolizing the conversation all evening, and not giving you a chance to talk. Very remiss of us.''

Samantha could cheerfully have strangled him. Brightly she said, ''You know me, I always have things to think about. Annie. Work. Things I wouldn't want to bore you with.''

''I'd like to hear about your work,'' Melissa said.

''Not tonight, Mel.'' Max turned to Samantha. ''Come, darling, time to go to our room.''

Melissa looked confused. ''When you said time for bed, I didn't think...''

''What didn't you think, Mel?''

''That the two of you were sharing a room.''

Max smiled at her. ''Didn't you?''

Samantha was about to say she wasn't tired, and that Max should go ahead without her. Before she could speak, Max took her hands and drew her to her feet. ''Come along, darling.'' His arm went around Samantha's shoulders, as he looked at his sister. ''Good night, Mel, see you tomorrow.''

Samantha did not trust herself to speak until the bedroom door was closed. ''Quite an act, Max,'' she said then.

''Is that what it was?''

''What else? Look, Max, I know this is necessary, but I'm not comfortable playing tricks on Melissa.''

He looked down at her, his eyes searching her face. ''You surprise me. It was your idea to move my things in here.''

She shifted beneath the smoldering intensity of his gaze. ''I know that.''

''You did it for Annie's sake. Or so you said.''

''Only for Annie's sake,'' Samantha snapped. ''Think Melissa believed us, Max?''

"I have no idea. My sister isn't a fool." He grinned at her. "Fact is, Melissa's visit brought me back to this room, and that's all that matters to me right now."

Samantha, her nerves already raw, felt her heart begin a rapid beating. "It doesn't mean a thing! Didn't I just tell you that? And we talked about it before dinner."

Max's grin became positively wicked. "Want to know what I remember of that discussion, Samantha? That we'll be sleeping in the same room—in the same bed—and that any consequences will take care of themselves."

Samantha gave a violent shake of her head. "It's not the way I understood it."

"I believe you will." His voice was soft now, spine-tinglingly seductive. "No sleeping on chairs for me, darling. I repeat, it was your idea for us to sleep together. You had to know you were playing with fire when you moved my things in here."

"I wasn't thinking about sex," she said wildly.

"How could you not, a woman who'd had a sex life like ours?"

"I told you the reason, Max. Melissa is here to spy on us. The situation called for desperate measures. Didn't you hear me?"

"I heard, darling. Doesn't mean I agreed. Don't have any illusions, Samantha, I've never believed in platonic bedmates."

Platonic? With Max filling the room with his maleness and virility, there was not a platonic nerve in Samantha's entire body. But she couldn't—wouldn't—give way to her feelings. She just wished she didn't have to keep reminding herself of that fact.

"Platonic relationships do exist," she said hoarsely.

Max laughed. "Not between you and me."

"As long as you don't think you can touch me," she muttered fiercely.

"Would you stop me?"

"I might decide to sleep in the den," Samantha said, knowing very well she would do nothing of the sort.

"With Melissa next door?" Max shook his head. "I don't think so. That would defeat the whole object of this exercise, wouldn't it?"

Eyes stormy, she looked at him. "In other words, I'm trapped."

In one of those familiar gestures she had always loved, Max's hands cupped her face. She knew she had to move away from him, and couldn't.

"You're only trapped if you think you are."

"I am trapped, Max. I don't have any choice but to let you sleep here with me—not if I put Annie's interests first."

Still cupping her face, he began to stroke her throat. After a moment he said, "You know I would never force you to do anything you didn't want to do."

"But you said…"

"I know what I said. You don't have to find another room, Samantha. I want to make love to you, all night if you'd let me. But if you convince me it's not what you want, I won't press you. I believe the day will come when you'll tell me what you really want."

With that she should have been content. Yet as Max's hands dropped away from her face, Samantha felt curiously disappointed and bereft. It was all so much easier when he took the lead. Now he was throwing the ball into her court, making it clear that henceforth she would have to take the initiative. Normally it wouldn't have been a problem. But with the memory of Edna pulling her one way, and her irresistible love for Max tugging her the other, she didn't know if she would ever have it in her to go begging.

Without another word, Max moved nonchalantly away from her and picked up his pajamas. Samantha's breathing grew shallow as he began to remove his clothes. When he took off his shirt, it was impossible for her to tear her eyes away from the sight of his bare chest, like burnished copper in the glow of the bedside light. Somehow she had to suppress the desire—an insane desire—to explore the hard curves of that chest with her fingers.

He was starting to unbuckle his belt when Samantha found the strength to move. Averting her eyes, she grabbed her nightie, and made for the bathroom. When she came back into the room, Max was already in bed. He chuckled as she slipped quickly beneath the blanket, and lay stiffly, as close as she could to the edge of the bed.

"Something funny, Max?"

"You. The way you're lying there, shrinking from me. As if you have no idea what sex is all about, as if you're terrified. Anyone would think you were a virgin, Samantha, instead of an intensely warm-blooded and very passionate woman. The one thing we always had in our marriage was fantastic sex."

That was exactly the problem. Their love life had indeed been fantastic—more exciting than anything she could have imagined before Max had introduced her to the ecstasies of physical pleasure. It was also true that she was passionate; this was what was making it so difficult for her now. If being in a car or a room with Max was hard, sharing a bed with him was going to be a very special kind of torture.

The fact that the bed was queen- rather than king-size, hadn't worried them in the past. Sleeping with their bodies curled into each other, they had never needed more space. Now Samantha was acutely aware of the male body so close to hers. Everything about Max inflamed her senses— his warmth, his male scent, his all-encompassing sexiness.

How would she manage to sleep, when sleep was the last thing on her mind? And how was it possible for Max to remain so calm? Perhaps because he was thinking of Edna, she thought numbly.

Lying on her side, with her face away from him, she said, "This isn't going to work."

"I don't see why not."

"You and me in one bed."

"You are the one who believes in platonic roommates." He was just close enough that she could feel his breath on her neck.

"Don't taunt me, Max!"

She jerked as an arm went around her waist. "What are you doing?" she snarled.

"Just being friendly," he said into her ear.

She swallowed hard over a throat that was suddenly dry. "You promised you wouldn't."

"I promised not to have sex with you unless you wanted it. Nobody said anything about not being friendly."

"You call this being *friendly?*"

Max slid across the small space separating them, his body curling around her. His arm held her even more closely. "What do you call it, my very beautiful wife?"

"A lot more than friendship." Her voice was ragged. "I wish you wouldn't do this, Max."

"Do what, darling? Hold you?"

His lips nuzzled the back of her neck, his teeth pulling slightly at the delicate skin.

"Don't, Max!" she cried hoarsely. "I can't bear it!"

His hand moved over her stomach, and then the tips of his fingers lightly touched her breasts beneath the thin fabric of the nightie. "Because," he asked softly, "you're thinking of Brian?"

Brian had never been further from her mind. "If I said yes?" she murmured.

"I wouldn't believe you."

She tried to lie still in the darkness, tried to ignore the evidence of Max's desire against her, and the throbbing and very primitive needs of her own body.

When she could speak, she whispered, "This isn't the first time you're flattering yourself."

The wicked fingers went higher, caressing her breasts and touching her nipples. "I'm just relying on my instincts, darling. Remembering how things used to be between us. I recognize the feel of you. Unless you've changed very much, I know what you like and need."

"I can't listen to this—*don't you understand?*"

Instead of answering, he kissed her throat again, first with his lips, then with two long brush-strokes of his tongue. In an instant, Samantha's body was on fire.

Max whispered, "You want this as much as I do. It's all there, just as it used to be. You're trembling, Samantha, and your nipples are hard. I know you so well, darling. You do your best to lie to me, but you've never been able to stop your body from telling the truth."

If she stayed in bed even one more second, with her body surrounded by his, she would weaken. Longing for him as she did, there was no way she would be able to go on resisting him. Throwing him off guard with her suddenness, Samantha jerked away from Max's arm, and leaped out of bed.

Running to the window, she stared unseeingly into the darkness, taking long breaths and willing her trembling to subside. It was a minute or so before Max came up behind her.

"Do you really hate me touching you?" He sounded troubled. "Could I have misread you so badly?"

There was no point in lying to him. In a low voice Samantha said, "You didn't misread me."

"You're saying you *do* want to make love?"

Without turning to him, she said unhappily, "Part of me does..."

"Samantha!" Max exclaimed joyfully.

Sensing that he was about to put his arms around her again, she moved away from him quickly. Somehow she forced herself to look at him. "Only one part, Max. The emotional part, the part I can't seem to control, the part that can't help responding to you."

"The part that matters, Samantha! The *only* part."

He was reaching for her, but she put out a hand to stop him. "No, Max. Because you see there's that other part— the thinking, rational part that tells me what a mistake it would be."

"You don't know what you're saying."

"I can't let you hurt me again, Max."

"I would *never* hurt you!" he declared passionately.

"Not physically. But you'll hurt me all the same—if I let you."

"Edna again." Max was clearly frustrated. "Can't we ever get beyond Edna?"

"You might be able to, I can't."

"You won't even let me talk about her."

"No," Samantha said with finality.

Max was silent for several seconds. In the moonlight that shone in through the window, Samantha saw that his face was hard, his lips tight.

"We have to get beyond this," he said at last.

"We can't."

"We must. You just admitted you still feel something for me." His voice was ragged.

"Physically," Samantha forced herself to say. "That's all it can ever be, Max. I can't feel anything else, not when I don't trust you—and I don't. I never will."

Max stepped away from her, as abruptly as if she had struck him. Looking at him, loving him desperately despite everything, Samantha almost let down her defences and went to him.

"Fine," Max said heavily, before she could move. "If that's how you feel, there's no point in us sharing a bed. We'll go on sharing the room while Melissa is here. For Annie's sake. But I'll take you up on your earlier suggestion—I'll put a few chairs together, and you can have the bed to yourself."

"Max..." she began.

"For the record," he said stonily, "one day I *will* have your trust."

CHAPTER SEVEN

IT WAS well past midnight when Samantha awoke. She lay still for a few seconds, staring into the darkness. Although she was half asleep, she was puzzled, for there was an emptiness in the room...as if something was missing.

Lifting herself on one elbow, she glanced across to the chairs that Max had been occupying for the last week or so, ever since Melissa's arrival. They were empty. She waited a few seconds, thinking he might have gone to the bathroom. When the minutes passed and he didn't return, she decided to investigate.

She left the room and walked down the hallway. The door to the den was slightly open, and even before she reached it, she saw that the light was on.

Max was at the desk, his forehead creased in concentration. Several thick folders lay open in front of him, and papers were scattered everywhere. He was typing, using two fingers.

"Max," she said from the doorway.

He looked up. "Samantha... Did I disturb you?"

"No. I woke up, and realized you weren't in the room."

She had once read that when people loved each other, a kind of sixth sense sometimes developed between them. It was the kind of thing that often happened with twins. She wouldn't tell Max that it had just happened to her: he would think her crazy if she did.

"What are you doing?"

He made a rueful face. "Working."

"I can see that. But at this time of night? For heaven's sake, Max, it's three in the morning! Can't it wait?"

"You're sounding like a wife."

But he was smiling, and as she smiled back at him, there was the kind of togetherness that had once been such an integral part of their relationship. Folding her arms over her chest, Samantha swallowed over the sudden lump in her throat. The last thing she wanted was to turn maudlin and sentimental, when what she really needed was to develop a hard shell that no pain could penetrate. Unfortunately there were things she could not seem to control, and loving Max was one of them.

"Imagine sounding like a wife, when I'm not." Samantha paused as an odd expression crossed Max's face. She waited for him to say something. When he didn't, she added, "Which doesn't stop me from wondering why you're sitting here at this time of night."

"It's this case. I have to be in court the day after tomorrow, and I'm nowhere near ready for it." Max shoved impatiently at some papers in front of him.

"You're usually so well organized."

"Not this time. Series of setbacks. Urgent matters coming in, and needing my attention. And then to top it all, my secretary taking ill at the very worst time."

"So you couldn't sleep because you were thinking of the case, and decided you'd better work on it."

"How well you know me."

"There are things I know... But you'll be exhausted if you keep on, Max. Can't it wait till morning?"

"Afraid not. I'll only go on lying awake thinking about it if I don't go on working now. Go to bed, Samantha. No point in both of us being exhausted, darling."

If only he wouldn't call her that. His endearments, meaningless though they were, would just make the inevitable parting more difficult. But this wasn't the time to take him up on it. Not when he looked so tired that his weariness caught at her heart.

Walking further into the room, she said, "I'll help you."

Max looked surprised. Standing, he came to her and touched her cheek. "No—but thanks for offering."

Her face was warm beneath his fingers, and she wanted nothing more than to lean her head against his chest. The last week had been the torture she'd expected. Sleeping in the same room as Max, yet deprived of the physical contact for which she hungered.

True to his word, he had not tried to make love to her again. Many was the time that Samantha had been tempted to make the first move, but always something had kept her back: pride, the anger that never left her, the knowledge that Edna—however discreet Max's behavior—was still a part of his life.

"I mean it, Max, I want to help. I saw you typing with two fingers. It'll take you forever like that. I'm a fast typist—remember?"

"Sure, I do."

"I used to help you in the past. No reason why I shouldn't help again now." Max's hand dropped from her face, leaving an empty space where it had been. "A very good reason," he said flatly. "Things have changed, as you keep reminding me. We're no longer married, not in the real sense of the word."

Samantha was unprepared for the pain that stabbed her. It was one thing for her to say the words, quite another to hear them from Max.

She tried to keep the pain from her expression. "Not a good enough reason. This hasn't anything to do with being married. I want to help. Two of us can get through the work much faster than one. If you dictate, and I type, we'll get through it in no time."

"You shouldn't have to do this," Max said.

"It's not a question of having to do it. I want to."

Max shook his head, but he was tempted, Samantha

knew: she had seen the expression that had appeared momentarily in his eyes. Following up on the brief advantage, she said, "We're wasting precious time."

"There's your job," he said slowly. "You'll need your sleep if you're going to work tomorrow." He grinned. "Make that today."

Samantha grinned back at him. "You're running out of excuses. I want to help you—don't you understand?"

"I'm beginning to."

"We always worked together well in the past."

Closing the distance between them, Max put his arms around her. "We did a lot of things well together in the past."

Samantha didn't answer him, nor did he seem to expect her to. His arms tightened around her, and she felt his lips move in her hair. As her heart began its familiar rapid beating, she couldn't resist nuzzling her mouth against the bare skin above the top button of his pajamas. She could have stood like this forever: Max's arms around her, the familiar male smell in her nostrils, the feeling that this was how they should always be.

All too soon, Max put her from him. "Not much more I can say. If you're really determined, let's get started."

She looked up at him, and as their eyes met, she saw an expression in his face that sent the blood racing in her veins. One eyebrow lifted and he looked at her quizzically, almost as if he was waiting for her to say something.

I love you. The words hovered on her lips. But she couldn't say them.

Instead she just said briskly, "You're right, we really should start."

She sat down on the chair by the computer, which Max had vacated, and he pulled up another chair opposite her at the desk. In no time, he was once more absorbed in his work. Since he was not yet ready to dictate, Samantha had a chance to watch him. After the brief moment of tenderness, he was all lawyer again, his mind juggling legalities, working out the tactics and strategies he intended using in court.

She had always enjoyed watching him when he worked. Max attracted her on every level. His hands, his body, his eyes and lips, all the things that went into his physical being, struck a chord deep inside her. But the razor-sharp workings of his mind appealed to her as well. She found his keen intelligence extraordinarily sexy.

He looked up suddenly, his eyes meeting hers again, and she knew he'd been aware of her scrutiny. Okay, Samantha, how about I give you some of the background to the case first?''

This was the part she had always loved best. The sense of being included in Max's work; the awareness that he was prepared to treat her as an intellectual equal, even though she had never studied law; the fact that he would make her part of a case instead of just expecting her to do his typing.

He began to tell her about the case, a complicated criminal suit involving millions of dollars. Max was acting for the plaintiff, a huge conglomerate that had fallen victim to sophisticated embezzlement and fraud. It was very important that he win this case.

Samantha listened intently as he spoke. Tired as Max was, he still had the knack of making the facts both interesting and believable. Samantha knew that no lawyer would present his client's side better than Max.

At length, he began to dictate. Samantha could type almost as fast as Max could speak. She didn't have to interrupt him, or ask him to repeat himself. Sometimes, she even rephrased a sentence in her own words.

They had been working almost an hour, when Max bundled his papers, stacked them neatly and put them back into their folders. "That's it," he announced. "You were an absolute godsend, Samantha. Without you, I'd have been sitting here till morning. I'd forgotten what a whiz you are at a keyboard.''

She glanced at him as they stood up and walked away from the desk. He looked so tired that she felt something wrench inside her once more. Without thinking, she touched his face, smoothing her thumb over his eyes.

She was about to drop her hand, when he caught it and brought it to his lips. He kissed the palm, first with his lips, and then with a small stabbing movement of his tongue. His eyes held hers all the while, defying them to move away. Samantha held her breath. It was a mystery to her that Max could be sexy even when he was exhausted.

''There are two things I want,'' he said, still holding her eyes. ''I'll let you make the choice.''

Her heart was beating fast. ''What are they?''

''I have this wild urge to make love to you.''

''And the other thing?'' she asked, wondering if he could feel the beat of her pulse in her hand.

''I'm starving.'' His eyes sparkled. ''Not nearly as exciting.''

Samantha laughed shakily. ''Two very human desires.''

''So what's your choice, Samantha?''

She didn't have to give it any thought. All she wanted was to go to bed with him. But she said, ''I'm hungry, too.''

They went to the kitchen and raided the refrigerator, taking out chicken, bread and mustard, and while Samantha made sandwiches, Max saw to the coffee. They took their midnight snack to the alcove in the corner.

''This is like old times,'' Max said. ''Remember how often we came down here in the middle of the night?''

''I remember,'' she said in a low voice. ''All those times we worked together, just like tonight.''

Max reached for her hand. "And sometimes we came down here after making love."

"Yes..."

"We made love more often than we worked." His voice had grown husky.

"We did." Her own voice shook.

He leaned toward her, so close to her now that his breath warmed her cheek. "We will again."

"Max...." She stopped, unable to go on.

"I know we will. Not tonight, maybe, but when you're ready for it." His thumb caressed the sensitive inner part of her wrist. "I know we will, Samantha."

Late as it was, Samantha did not fall asleep when her head touched the pillow. She felt wound up, anything but tired. The sound of Max's slow breathing filled the room, but her own mind was full of the warmth and intimacy of that half hour in the kitchen, making it impossible for her to sleep. It was one of those memories, she knew, that would remain with her for a long time after she had left this house.

At work the next morning, Samantha said to Hugh Rowland, "Would you mind if I took off tomorrow instead of the day after?"

"Sure, why not?" The Tweedle brothers were always affable. "Do you have plans with Annie?"

"Actually I was thinking of going into the city. My husband will be in court, and I'd like to be there."

"I don't blame you. Max Anderson is one top-notch lawyer, so I've heard. Must be great to watch him strut his stuff."

Samantha felt a warm glow of pride and pleasure at the admiration in Hugh's tone. It was one thing for her to think Max was special, something else again when an outsider confirmed it.

During dinner that evening, Max told Melissa how Samantha helped him the previous night. His sister seemed amazed, as if she found it hard to believe that Samantha would actually give up several hours of sleep to help her husband. Together with her surprise, there was also an unusual glimmer of respect. It was an expression that Samantha had noticed once or twice in the past week—almost as if her sister-in-law was beginning to regard her with different eyes.

Busy with her own thoughts, Samantha listened quietly while they talked. She hadn't made up her mind whether to tell Max she would be in court. In the early years of their marriage, she had gone to watch him once or twice, but she hadn't made a habit of it, thinking it might make him uptight if he knew she was there.

This time, however, she was drawn as if by a magnet to the courtroom. There had been something special about the night they had shared, something that was in its own way almost as intimate as their lovemaking. After typing Max's notes, Samantha felt as if she had a personal stake in the case. More than anything, she wanted to see Max perform before a judge and jury one more time before she left him—and this might well be her last chance.

By the time they were drinking their after-dinner coffee, she had made up her mind. She wouldn't tell him she was coming. She would surprise him.

"Wish me luck?" Max said as he left the breakfast table the next morning.

Wish me luck… The words he had always used before a big case. Words that were one more part of the fabric of their marriage. It was at times like these that Samantha felt as if nothing had changed.

"You're so well prepared you don't need to depend on luck, but here's some anyway." So saying, she picked up the salt and threw a few grains over each of Max's shoulders. She couldn't have said where the superstition had originated—but this, too, had become part of their ritual.

As she watched Max drive away, Samantha wondered whether she was doing the right thing in going to court. Perhaps there had been just a little too much intimacy in the past day or two. Besides, Max might not like it. But by the time she had taken Annie to kindergarten, she had gotten over her indecision. For once, she would follow the dictates of her heart rather than her head.

Racing back to the house, she hurried upstairs to her bedroom. She dressed quickly, but with special care, putting on the pearl-gray suit that she kept for special occasions. A dusty pink blouse softened the formality of the suit, and silver hooped earrings completed her appearance.

Before leaving the house, she made certain Helen would be picking up Annie at noon. "You look wonderful," the housekeeper said.

Melissa was still in her room, and Samantha was glad she wasn't around to ask questions. As it was, she was nervous enough as she left the house and drove to the station from where she caught the train into Manhattan.

Court was about to begin when she got there. The courtroom was crowded with newspaper reporters, as well as onlookers drawn by the media attention given to the case. Samantha was lucky to get a seat in the front row of the spectators' gallery, from where she would have an excellent view of the proceedings. Max was there already, tall and broad-shouldered and looking very distinguished. He was talking to a colleague, their heads bent over some documents.

He hadn't noticed her yet.

The jury members took their seats, and everyone in the courtroom rose to their feet as the judge entered. And then the proceedings began, and Max stood up once more and began to speak. The case had been going on for a week, but it could end today, which made for a sense of hushed expectancy.

"Isn't that lawyer a hunk?" whispered the woman beside Samantha.

"My husband," she whispered back quietly, her cheeks flushed with pride.

It was only when her neighbor looked at her with a mixture of envy and admiration that she remembered that Max wasn't her husband in any real sense of the word, that in a few months from now he wouldn't be her husband at all.

Unfortunately she seemed to be falling more deeply in love with him every day, and as her love intensified, so did her state of growing unreality. She had better get a grip on herself, Samantha told herself firmly—if she didn't, she could really fall apart when the time came to leave Max.

Sitting forward in her seat, she listened intently as he presented his arguments. His tone, always vital, was low when the things he was saying were purely legal, passionate when he felt strongly. But Max was a lawyer rather than a showman. He needed no histrionics to impress the jury, in fact he disdained unnecessary drama. He was impressing them all the same. Samantha could see the raptness in their faces, and sensed that the case was going his way.

An hour had passed when, for some reason, Max turned his head, and out of the crowd of faces in the gallery, he saw Samantha. Their eyes met and held for a long moment. To say that Max was surprised would have been an understatement. He looked absolutely astonished. And then he winked at her, the merest flicker of an eyelid, which few strangers would have registered.

As Max went on speaking, Samantha was filled with elation. She had been a bit nervous about coming here today, and had almost turned away on the steps of the courthouse.

But it was all right: Max didn't mind that she was here; if anything he had seemed pleased to see her.

She was particularly excited about the things he was saying now. She recognized his arguments for they were part of the work they had done together. Listening to him elaborate on the points he had made in the stillness of the den made her feel part of the case.

He didn't look at her again until he was finished, and then he turned, quite deliberately, and looked at her once more. She smiled at him, and for a moment it was as if they were the only ones in the courtroom. No judge or jury, no spectators—only the two of them: Max and Samantha, finishing what they had begun in the loneliness of the night.

The two legal teams presented their closing arguments, and then the judge sent the jury out to deliberate. Samantha was leaving her seat, when her neighbor stopped her. "Won't take them long to reach a verdict. Not after the way your hubby spoke. Lucky you—he's really something, isn't he?"

As Samantha left the courtroom, she saw Max conferring with his clients. Not wanting to interrupt, she hung back, but he saw her almost immediately, excused himself, and came to her.

"Why didn't you tell me you were coming?"

"Do you mind?"

"I'm delighted. Especially after all the work you did."

Taking her by the arm, he led her to his clients, and introduced her.

"Mrs. Anderson," said one of the men. "Good to meet you. If we lose this case, it won't be your husband's fault. He's done a superb job."

"Couldn't have done it without my wife," Max said, and told them how she had got up in the middle of the night to help him.

Samantha flushed with pleasure—the last thing she had

expected was that Max would give her credit. He had to go back to his office then, and she made her way back to the station.

"You look very pleased with yourself," Melissa said when Samantha walked into the house. "You don't usually go to work dressed like that. Been somewhere special?"

Samantha hesitated a moment, but she couldn't keep the truth from her sister-in-law. "Actually I went to watch Max's case."

Melissa's eyebrows drew together in a frown. "You shouldn't have done that! Lawyers hate their families to watch them in court."

"I don't think that's necessarily so," Samantha said lightly.

"Believe me it is," Melissa said feelingly. "When Dad was cross-examining, he wouldn't have allowed me within a mile of the courtroom. Pity you didn't ask me, Samantha, I'd have warned you. Don't be surprised if Max is really mad."

But Max was anything but mad with her. She followed him up to the bedroom when he came home from work, and watched as he took off his jacket and loosened his tie.

"Were you upset that I was in court?" she asked.

"Good Lord, no! Why would you think that? Didn't you see I was glad?"

"I did think you were, but I wanted to make sure. I believe lawyers don't always welcome their families in court."

"Some lawyers do find it a bit inhibiting to have their nearest and dearest around when they're arguing a case. But not this lawyer, and definitely not this case. Especially after all you did. I was *glad* you were there, Samantha. Made me sharper, just knowing you were there listening. Kept me on my toes."

Samantha laughed happily. "Now you're talking nonsense. But I admit I enjoyed hearing you elaborate on all those points you dictated. It was all so different from the way it sounded in the middle of the night."

"Meaning you approved?"

She slanted him a teasing look. "At the risk of increasing the size of your head—I guess I understand why people think you're a good lawyer."

Max cupped her face in his hands. "Thanks for the evaluation. But I'm still waiting for that other evaluation."

"Which one is that?"

"The personal one."

Samantha's breathing quickened. "Am I supposed to know what you're talking about?"

"I'm still waiting to be your lover."

"Max…"

"No jury will tell me how I perform in your bed. Only you, Samantha. Only you, darling." One thumb brushed up and down her throat, the other closed over her lips. "You don't have to answer, not now. But soon, Samantha. Make it very soon."

Samantha remained silent, because at that moment there was only one answer she could have given him, and she knew she would regret it afterward. Just as well, she thought, that Melissa and Annie were waiting for them at the supper table. Her heart would have given him the answer long ago. But it was in her head that the real answer had to be formulated, and right now her head was no more reliable than her heart.

Max called her from the courthouse a few days later. "Jury's going to be handing down the verdict three hours from now. Can you be here?"

The Tweedle Brothers, Samantha's amiable bosses, were

quite happy to let her rearrange her schedule again. Sure, they told her, take the day off and enjoy the courtroom drama. Gratefully she promised to work the whole of the next week in return.

She got ready in record time, managing to be in court before the proceedings started. Max must have been looking out for her, because he came to her a few minutes after she sat down, touched her arm and said so softly that only she could hear him, "I'm glad you're here."

Flushed with pleasure, she whispered back, "I wouldn't have missed it. Good luck."

He left her then, and not long after that the judge and jury entered the courtroom. Max looked at her for a second, and as their eyes met she gave him a quick thumbs-up signal. He turned back to the jury then, and there was a hush in the courtroom as the jury foreman began to read. The hush lasted a few seconds after the verdict had been given. Then an animated buzz erupted, which was silenced immediately by the judge.

Max had won. Samantha sat motionless, barely aware of the reactions of the people all around her—those who were glad, and those who were inevitably bitterly disappointed. All she knew was that Max, her beloved Max, had won the case on which he had worked so hard.

The judge was speaking now. The jury had given their decision. It remained for him to determine the penalties, and he would do this when he had had a chance to consider the issues. After thanking the jury for their efforts, he released them from their duties. Then he, too, left the courtroom.

The judge's departure was the signal for the noise to resume. Max was on his feet now, and people were congratulating him. His clients were thumping him on the back, as were his colleagues. The case had aroused so much interest, that several lawyers who happened to be in the court-house at the time had come to listen to the verdict.

Samantha waited, uncertain whether this was the time to approach Max. This was his world, and until now she had never had any part in it..

Suddenly he was at her side. "We did it," he said.

Samantha laughed up at him. "*You* did it! You did it, Max."

"We." He said the word again. "I couldn't have managed without your help."

He was talking nonsense, of course, yet she couldn't help being extraordinarily happy that he was once again giving her credit for helping him.

By now people were closing in on him again, so that there was no time for further private comments. All she could say was, "Congratulations. See you at home."

She watched him walk away with his little entourage of lawyers and clients, knowing that her time with him would come later. And then she, too, was leaving the courthouse.

It was still early, an hour or so before noon, and Samantha wondered what do with herself. She could catch the train back to Long Island, and be home in time to pick up Annie. But Helen had said she would do that, and after lunch Helen was going to be taking the little girl to a birth-day party. So really, there was no hurry for Samantha to go back.

For a while she wandered through the busy streets, win-dow-shopping rather than doing any actual buying. She was saving her money as diligently as ever, even though Max had on more than one occasion told her to buy whatever she wanted. Knowing that their marriage was only a cha-rade, she had no intention of spending his money on her-self. When she did buy something, it was almost always for Annie.

But today was different, today she had an urge to buy something for Max. Feeling unusually extravagant, she chose a lovely tiepin. When she had had it gift-wrapped, she bought a card, wrote a few words and taped it to the outside of the package. She would give it to him after dinner, she decided.

A different thought struck her seconds later. Why not take Max out to lunch?

A cab took her to Wall Street, and then she caught an elevator to the 53rd floor of the building where Max worked. The receptionist had been there for years, and she greeted Samantha warmly. "Mrs. Anderson. It's been a while."

"It has, Brenda. Nice to see you again."

They chatted a minute or two, and when Samantha had enquired after Brenda's children, she asked, "Is Max with a client?"

"I don't think so. Should I buzz through and tell him you're here?"

"No need, thanks. I think I'll just surprise him."

The door with the brass plate that was now engraved with Max's name instead of his father's was slightly ajar. Samantha pushed it open, and took a step into the office—only to stop abruptly.

Max and Edna stood by the desk. Edna's arms were folded around Max's neck, his hands were on her waist. As Samantha stood there, frozen in shock, Edna's head tilted upward for a kiss.

CHAPTER EIGHT

NEITHER Max nor Edna had seen her.

For a moment that seemed frozen in time, Samantha simply stood there. She was unable to speak, to move. She felt ill. When she could think again, her impulse was to turn and leave before the other two saw her. Apart from the receptionist, nobody would ever know she had been here, and she wouldn't tell Brenda what had happened. She could retreat and save face, and neither Max nor Edna would ever be the wiser.

Three times now she had surprised Max, and two of those times had turned into disasters. Would she never learn?

She had taken a step backward, when her first impulse was replaced by a second. *Face-saving be damned!* She had done enough of that; she was not going to do it again. No matter the consequences.

She tapped the door lightly. Two heads jerked around in surprise.

"Samantha!" Max looked stunned.

In Edna's face, surprise was mixed with venomous triumph. Her arms remained twined around Max's neck.

"Am I interrupting something?" Samantha asked, with deliberate lightness.

"No." Max detached himself from Edna. Moving away from the woman, he said, "Edna just came to congratulate me."

Samantha was determined to play things very cool. "Congratulations—yes, I see. The same thing I'm here for."

133

"You weren't announced." Edna sounded belligerent.

"I didn't think I had to be." Samantha threw her a somewhat disdainful look. With heavier emphasis, she added, "After all, I'm Max's *wife*."

"True," Max said.

"But still... The receptionists know better than to let all and sundry go wandering through the offices."

"Samantha is hardly all and sundry," Max said quietly. "And she's right, she *is* my wife."

"Who has come to take you to lunch." Amazed at her own brazenness and determination to fight, Samantha smiled at him. "After your triumph in the courtroom, I hope you can take off half an hour?"

"I can do better than that. Let's make it an hour."

"Max!" The triumph had gone from Edna's face: she was flushed and angry now. "Are you forgetting that Discovery? It's due on Thursday—we were going to work on it during lunch."

"It will have to wait," Max told her, with a firmness that gave Samantha no end of satisfaction.

Cool, stay cool, she reminded herself, and managed to keep a smile on her face as she walked out of the office with Max. She was aware that Edna was glowering at them both, and this added to her satisfaction. The sick feeling was still there, a constant presence in her chest and her stomach, but she was damned if she was going to let either of them know it.

The restaurant they went to was one where Max seemed to be well-known. People kept stopping him, some just to say hello, others to congratulate him on his success in court. Even the waiter treated him with deference, and although the place was crowded, they were given a plum alcove table.

They made small talk, mainly about the case, until the waiter had taken their order. Samantha was amazed that she could converse so calmly, when her mind was buzzing with anger.

"About Edna—" Max began, when the waiter had gone.

"When will you learn that I don't want to talk about her?"

"But we have to talk." Max was frowning. "You saw Edna and me together, and next thing you'll be walking out on me again like the last time. That's why—"

"Actually I have no intention of walking out." Samantha threw him a deliberately provocative look.

"Do you mean that?" He was eyeing her warily.

"Absolutely."

"And you don't want any explanations?"

"I told you I didn't."

"What's got into you, Samantha?" Max asked cautiously.

His embarrassment fractionally lessened her anger. It was wonderful to see Max at a disadvantage for a change.

"Are you saying you don't care any longer? Is that what you're saying, Samantha?"

If he only knew! There was a place deep inside her that was twisted and wrenched with pain at the mental picture of Edna and Max about to launch into a passionate kiss. But she would not let him know it. The old insecure ways hadn't worked for her in the past—she was going to play her cards very differently this time.

"The conversation is becoming a little boring, Max."

"Boring!" he exclaimed, with feeling.

"Well, yes. Edna, always Edna. I didn't stay over in the city just to talk about Edna."

"Why did you stay?"

"To take you to lunch," she said, outwardly cheerful.

"That's all there is to it?"

"And to congratulate you."

Max's eyes were dark and brooding as they moved over her face. Samantha forced herself to sit very still as he studied her. Beneath the tablecloth her hands gripped each other tightly; she was trying with every ounce of her strength to maintain her composure. But maintain it she did, because she was determined to play the part she had chosen for herself.

"I don't understand," Max said abruptly.

"Really? And I thought it was so simple. You just won a very important case, and I wanted to wish you well."

"I'm not talking about the case, and you damn well know it! It's you, Samantha. I don't understand you."

Samantha kept her expression bland, hiding her pleasure. "I didn't realize there was anything *to* understand."

"You're acting out of character, dammit, and I want to know why."

"Maybe you don't know me as well as you thought you did, Max," she said breezily.

"Maybe not."

Max took a bread roll from a basket on the table, and began tearing it with unusual fierceness. His eyes were bleak, his lips hard. Watching him, Samantha was quiet. Men were such contrary beings, she thought wryly. It was just fine for her husband to have a mistress on the side: obviously he didn't give a second thought to the fact that he was cheating on Samantha. But for some reason, it seemed to bother him that she no longer minded. It was something she didn't understand, but she had no intention of asking him about it.

The waiter arrived with their drinks, and she lifted her glass, smiled and said, "Congratulations."

"Thanks."

"You were great in court. I'm not surprised the jury found for your client."

"Thanks," he said again.

"I wouldn't have missed it for the world."

"I'm glad you were there." Max looked ill at ease, as though he was still wondering why she was behaving so differently from the way he would have expected.

"I have something for you." Samantha took the small gift-wrapped package from her purse.

"A present?" He was surprised.

"Yes—aren't you going to open it?"

"When I've read the card."

For a man who spent his days reading long and complicated documents, often at great speed, Max seemed to be taking an extraordinarily long time to read the few lines on the card. Samantha watched him, wondering what he was thinking.

He looked up and searched her face. "Thanks for the nice words. I only wish..." He stopped.

Samantha decided not to help him out. Instead, into the small silence, she said, "Are you going to look at your gift?"

She watched as he tore the paper, and opened the box. For what seemed like a long time he looked down at the tiepin, before taking it from its velvet bed.

"Do you like it?" she asked, determined to keep any anxiety from her tone.

"It's beautiful," Max said roughly. "I love it. And I—" Again he stopped.

A little tensely, Samantha waited for him to finish the sentence. But he didn't go on with it, didn't say the words she so desperately longed to hear from him. Instead he reached across the table and took one of her hands in his.

"I'd give anything for you not to have seen me with Edna." His voice was low and rough.

"Max—"

"I know you don't want me to talk about her, and we won't—even though there are things I really need to say to you.'' His fingers tightened around her wrist. ''Thank you for this lovely gift. It means more to me than I can tell you, darling.''

Wretched man! Enjoying his time with his mistress, and believing that he could follow up with a lot of nonsense to his wife, and actually have her believe him. The trouble was, he looked so sincere—brilliant actor that he was—but with so many people around who knew him, this was not the right time for a dressing-down. Besides, she had to remember to play things coolly—at least for now.

She was glad when their food arrived: crepes filled with mushrooms cooked in a herbed cream sauce. The waiter uncorked a bottle of white wine, and poured a little into Max's glass; when he had nodded his approval, he filled Samantha's glass.

Amazingly, in the circumstances, they were actually able to talk, perhaps because the wine helped to loosen their tongues. The one topic that didn't come up again was Edna. This wasn't to say that Samantha didn't think about Max's mistress, she did. She had seen them together—again, and she knew she finally had to do something about their affair. But she would only act when she was ready.

When she looked at her watch, she couldn't believe the time. ''Two o'clock!'' she exclaimed in astonishment.

''You didn't tell me you had another appointment,'' Max teased.

''I don't—but you do. That Discovery you're supposed to be working on...with Edna.''

''It'll have to wait until later. Actually,'' Max said, ''I do have an appointment. With a lawyer two blocks from here. So if you're just about ready to go...'' He signaled to the waiter for the bill.

He wanted to pay, but Samantha reminded him that the lunch had been her idea. She insisted on paying, and although the amount would make quite a dent in her savings—savings she would soon be needing—the feeling of independence she derived from laying out her own money was worth every cent.

At the door of the restaurant, they parted. As Samantha watched Max walk away in the opposite direction from the building where his offices were located, it occurred to her that she hadn't shown jealousy, anger or insecurity even once since the moment she had found Edna and Max in each other's arms.

Edna looked up from a pile of papers. "So... Samantha... At least, this time you had the sense to go through the receptionist." She paused. "If you're looking for Max—he isn't here."

Samantha gave a cool smile. "I know that. I've just left him."

"You had lunch till *now?* It's two hours since he left the office!"

"Does my husband have to clock in with you?"

"Don't be ridiculous," Edna snapped. "But two hours is a long time for a social lunch."

"I didn't chain him down, if that's what you're implying," Samantha said sweetly. "We had lots to talk about, and the time just flew."

Edna threw her a poisonous look. Pointedly she picked up a few papers. "Nice to be a lady of leisure. But I'm very busy, so I hope you're not here to waste my time."

Ignoring the hint, the new cool Samantha walked further into the office. For a moment she debated whether to sit down in the chair at Edna's desk, but decided she was better off standing.

Looking directly at Edna, she said, "I haven't come here for social small talk. When I've said what I have to, I'll leave."

"Get to the point," Edna snarled.

Now that the moment had come, Samantha hesitated. She was suddenly very conscious of the fact that Edna was way out of her league. Not only was she brilliantly competent, but she was also stunning to look at. No wonder Max was bowled over by her.

For a second or two she asked herself if she had been crazy to come here. What had made her think, even for a moment, that anything she could say would stir Edna's conscience?

She was actually tempted to turn tail and leave Edna's office, when her anger came to her rescue. It was that anger that had carried her through the past two hours in the restaurant with Max, and it would stand her in good stead now. She was here to do battle with Edna, and she was damned if she was going to walk out without giving it her best shot.

"Leave my husband alone."

Edna had the grace to look startled. "What did you say?"

"You heard me the first time. It's time you stopped running after my husband."

The startled look was replaced by a blatant sneer. "Is that what I'm doing?"

"Don't act innocent with me, Edna. This isn't the first time we've talked. I wish now I'd been more outspoken at the Langleys' cocktail party. I should have given you an ultimatum then."

"An ultimatum?" Edna laughed. "What kind of ultimatum, Samantha? What do you think you can possibly do to me?"

Samantha didn't know the answer to the question. Ultimatums were useless, she realized, when her husband was such a willing partner in the relationship with this detestable woman. But she had come too far to retreat now.

"I don't have to go into details," she said quietly. "The

fact is, I won't have you carrying on with Max. I am not prepared to take it any longer.''

Edna laughed again—a rough, unpleasant sound that grated on Samantha's frayed nerves. ''Well, well, well— whatever happened to the timid little mouse? The one who ran away when she caught me in bed with her husband? Who made an excuse to leave the party early when she didn't like the things I said? The mouse who couldn't take a little bit of competition?''

Samantha's anger was fast boiling into fury. ''This isn't the first time you've called me a mouse. Don't do it again!''

''You didn't stop me the last time.'' Edna sneered. ''What's different this time? Are you telling me the mouse has changed into a dragon?''

An ornamental paperweight lay on the desk. Samantha picked it up without thinking. It felt cool and hard in her hand. It felt lethal. Edna's eyes met hers in a mocking look.

''You wouldn't have the courage to throw it at me,'' the lawyer said.

''It's amazing the things people will do when they're goaded. But you're right, I wouldn't throw this thing.'' Samantha put the paperweight back on the desk. ''Not only because I don't fancy criminal charges, but I don't believe in physical violence—it doesn't solve anything.''

''You really have changed,'' Edna said. ''Where did the fierceness come from? Or was it always there?''

''It's new,'' Samantha informed her. ''And long overdue. So stop thinking of me as a mouse, Edna, I'm not.''

''A dragon?'' That unpleasant laugh again.

Taking a breath, Samantha placed her hands flat on the desk and looked directly into the other woman's eyes. ''Not a dragon, either. Just a woman in love with her husband, and determined to fight to keep him.''

There! She had said it. She had made a public declaration of her love for Max. She had also thrown out a challenge.

"Well!" A new expression had appeared in the lawyer's face: a mixture of surprise and anger and even—could it be?—respect.

"You're only going to be with Max for six months," Edna said thoughtfully.

"The period isn't written in stone. I can stay as long as I like. Anyway, that's not something I intend discussing with you."

"Does Max know you might stay on longer?"

"My discussions with my husband are private." Unless, of course, Max decided to repeat them to Edna, which Samantha could only hope he did not.

Edna was quiet a moment. "Is there a point to all this?" she asked at last.

"I thought I'd made the point. I want you out of Max's life. I can't do anything about what happened in the past. My only concern now is the present. Max is my husband, and I have no intention of sharing him with you."

Edna stood up and went to the window. She stood there for at least a minute, looking out across the skyscrapers. Samantha watched her tensely, wondering what was going on in her head. Would she agree to give Max up? Even more to the point, would Max give her up? But Samantha could only deal with one issue at a time, and right now she was dealing with Edna.

At length, Edna turned. "Did you say you love Max?"

"Very much."

"Enough to fight for him—is that really what you said?"

"Better believe it!" Samantha spoke with unusual fierceness.

"Why didn't you fight the first time? When you found him in bed with me?"

Samantha shrugged. "I should have. But that's water under the bridge now."

Looking at Edna, she wished she could read the strange expression in the other woman's eyes. There was something here that she didn't understand, and it was making her uneasy.

"What would you do if you found us in bed again?"

The question was so unexpected that Samantha was taken back. But she answered Edna sturdily. "Throw your clothes out of the window. Give you exactly one minute to go down after them."

Edna's eyes glinted. "You really have changed."

"I hope I've answered the question."

"In a way you have."

Samantha waited a few seconds, wondering if Edna meant to elaborate on her statement. When she didn't, she said, "Actually I don't really know what I'd do. But I can tell you one thing—I would fight you in any way I could."

"In other words, you've become a worthy competitor."

The words were so unexpected that Samantha could only stare at Edna in amazement. "What are you saying? This isn't a game."

"Isn't it? Actually it's a game in which the dynamics have changed. I guess you could say it just became more interesting."

"Does it matter that I don't know what you're talking about?"

Edna sat down at her desk again, and motioned Samantha to sit, too.

Samantha remained standing. "I've said what I wanted. I'll be on my way now."

"Sit. It's my turn to say something." Edna sounded impatient.

A hard knot of tension had formed in Samantha's stomach. Clearly Edna had something on her mind. All she could think of was that the woman was going to tell her that she and Max were privately engaged, that they were only waiting for the six months to end, for the divorce to proceed and become final, so that they could be married.

"Something I think you'll be glad to hear." Despite the reassuring words, there was an unmistakable glint of malice in Edna's eyes. "Now, will you sit?"

Dreading what was coming, Samantha sat down reluctantly.

"About the night you caught us in bed." Edna paused deliberately, before going on. "You assumed we were making love."

Samantha was rigid in an instant. "Weren't you?"

"No."

Samantha stared at the lawyer in disbelief. "Give me a break! You were lying there, stark naked. Max—" her voice shook "—Max was with you."

"Your darling husband was wearing pajamas. Or don't you remember?" Edna's tone was heavy with sarcasm.

"But I thought…"

"Wrongly." Still the sarcasm. "I'm not saying *I* didn't want to make love. Of course I did…that's why I was there. Naked and available in Max's bed."

Edna picked up a pencil and began to doodle on a piece of paper in front of her. Samantha sat stiffly on the edge of her chair, hardly breathing as she waited for her to continue.

Putting down the pencil, Edna looked up. "I was in a relationship that had just ended. Brutally, without any warning. I felt as if my world had ended, I was hurting like all hell. And there was Max, good-looking, dynamic, without a doubt the sexiest man at the conference. I needed a man at that moment. Badly. Someone to have sex with, someone to make me feel I was still desirable. I had to know I was still an attractive woman."

"Didn't you think you could be hurting someone else?"

Samantha whispered into the small silence that followed Edna's last words. "Didn't you feel guilty?"

"Guilty? Hell, no!" Edna's voice was hard. "When a man ditches you, you're not thinking of anyone else. I wanted Max. You weren't there, and I didn't see what possible harm there could be if I spent a night with him."

"You didn't think of me?" Despite her resolve to remain cool, Samantha was trembling.

"You didn't enter my mind."

"And so you invited my husband to have sex with you," Samantha said bitterly, thinking *he didn't have to accept.*

"It wasn't quite like that. I managed to get into his room. I was naked in the bed when he came in. There was only a light in the corner of the room, and he didn't see me at first. I have to admit, I didn't exactly make myself visible. Max had had a few drinks by then, and was a bit smashed. He was in his pajamas, getting into bed, before he knew I was there."

Once again, she paused. Samantha was so tense that her stomach muscles hurt. She didn't want to hear the rest of the story, and knew that she had to.

"I threw myself at him. Literally. Max wasn't interested. Do you know what that did for my self-esteem? Rejected first by one man, then another?"

Samantha didn't care about Edna's self-esteem. Rejected—that was the word that caught her. "You're saying Max rejected you?"

"Your precious husband said no to my offer. I tried to seduce him. He wasn't interested. Want to know what he said? He said he was married, and in love with his wife."

Samantha looked at the lawyer in shock. After dreading what she was going to hear, it was hard to take in the full implications of the story Edna was telling her.

"And that's when I arrived?" she whispered, when she could speak.

"Not quite then. Max realized how distraught I was, and being one hell of a guy, he didn't throw me out of bed. He held me in his arms, and let me talk and cry. When I had finished crying, and was trying once more to seduce him, he asked me to leave. *That* was when you barged into the room."

"My God!" Samantha exclaimed, horrified.

"You should have seen your face, " Edna said mockingly. "You looked as if you were going to faint on the spot."

"After what you'd just been through, I'd have thought you'd have some sympathy for me," Samantha accused.

"You didn't wait for sympathy, honey. Max tried to talk to you, but you wouldn't listen. You just ran out of that room as if a million demons were after you. Just like that little mouse I keep comparing you to. You refused to let Max explain."

"*You* could have told me."

"Why would I? You wouldn't listen to your husband, and God knows, he apparently tried often enough to talk to you. So why would I talk to you? By then, I was beginning to fall for the guy myself. Max Anderson is pretty terrific, in case you haven't noticed, Samantha."

"I've noticed," she said grimly. "I told you, I intend fighting for him. But I still don't understand, Edna, why are you telling me all this now? I realize—kind of—why you didn't say anything that night in the hotel room. I'd caught you off guard. But at the Langleys' party—you could have said something then. Instead you were so sarcastic. You implied you were having an affair with Max. What's different now?"

"The difference is in you, Samantha."

Edna's eyes searched her face, still with no hint of liking.

Her hostility was as strong as ever. But the glimmer of respect that Samantha had glimpsed earlier was present again now.

"As I told you—for the first time I'm seeing you as a worthy opponent. When you behaved like a frightened rabbit, I had nothing but contempt for you. I didn't think you deserved Max, didn't feel he should be saddled with you. But when you barged in here, ready to fight, I realized I had to give you a second chance."

"I guess I should be thanking you." Hard to believe she was actually saying these words.

Edna laughed. "Skip the thanks, lady. If you think I've given up on Max, you're mistaken. I'll be available, anytime he wants me. He's a great guy...the greatest I know."

"In which case, I'm wondering why you decided to tell me the truth."

"I figured you'd earned the right to know."

"Thanks..."

"I told you, skip it." Edna gestured dismissively. "Now will you please get the hell out of my office. I have work to do."

CHAPTER NINE

"SAMANTHA? *Samantha!*"

She looked up, aware for the first time that Melissa had been talking to her, and knowing she hadn't heard a thing that was said.

"I was making a toast to Max," said her sister-in-law. "To congratulate him on the case."

Samantha lifted her glass, smiling at Max as she echoed Melissa's toast. "Your brother was amazing in court."

"She's exaggerating," said a smiling Max. "I was lucky more than anything else."

"Luck had nothing to do with it," Samantha said firmly.

They drank their wine, and then Melissa said, "You've been preoccupied all evening. Something on your mind, Samantha?"

"No—well at least nothing important," she lied.

But Melissa was right. The conversation at the dinner table had washed right over her, so that she couldn't have said what Max and his sister had been talking about.

Over and over, the words went through her mind. *Max loved her. Max hadn't cheated on her. She loved Max, and Max loved her.* The words had been drumming inside her since the moment she'd left Edna's office several hours earlier. Through the cab ride to Penn Station, on the train to Long Island, driving the car back to the house, the words hadn't left her for a second.

Max loved her, had always loved her. He had tried to tell her about Edna, but she had interrupted him every time. A year of their lives had been wasted because she had refused to listen when he wanted to talk. Instead she had insisted on going ahead with a divorce that never should have been instigated in the first place.

All this was about to change. She couldn't wait to see Max's face when she told him that she knew the truth. But there was something else they were going to do first, something they would do before they talked.

"You're not in bed," Max said, when he walked into the bedroom a while later.

"No."

"Usually you're asleep when I come in, although sometimes I wonder..."

"Wonder what?" Samantha asked softly.

"Whether you're only pretending to—" He stopped abruptly, the words seeming to stick in his throat as Samantha came toward him.

She heard the sharp intake of his breath as his eyes moved over her, hungrily, greedily, as if he couldn't believe what he was seeing. His gaze was so intense that Samantha could almost feel it caressing her shoulders and breasts, where the spaghetti straps of the minuscule nightie left her skin bare.

"My God!" he exclaimed. "You look incredible!"

"Do I?" The flirtatious tone was one she hadn't used for so long that it sounded foreign to her ears.

His look of utter disbelief made every penny she'd spent on the nightie—the outrageous amount in direct disproportion to the scantness of the garment—worthwhile.

"Incredible! Gorgeous!" A small pause. "I wish I understood."

Heart racing, Samantha smiled at him. "What don't you understand, Max?"

"I thought you'd be mad at me. Finding Edna in my office like that. We had a great lunch, but I wondered if I'd get home and find you packing your suitcases again."

"Even brilliant men are sometimes wrong." She was still flirting with him, and loving every moment.

His hands went to her shoulders, cradling them in his fingers. "What's this all about, darling?"

His fingers were warm and vibrant, making her tremble with longing. She loved Max so much, and it frightened her to think how close she had come to losing him.

"Don't you recognize seduction when you see it?" she asked softly.

"Seduction?" Max repeated hoarsely.

"Seduction, yes, Max," she whispered, directing her words upward to his lips.

"You want me to make love to you?" Still that same hoarse tone. Samantha, who knew him so well, sensed that Max was just barely in control of himself.

"So many questions." She gave a ragged laugh. "I'm beginning to wonder if you really want to."

"You don't mean that!"

"Max... You said you wouldn't try to make love until I asked you to. Well...I'm asking you now."

"Samantha! I hope I'm not dreaming."

"You're not dreaming," she said jerkily. "An invitation, Max—are you going to take me up on it?"

"*Am I ever!*" Holding her a little away from him, he looked down at her. "You've never invited me before, darling. Not once. Not even in the good times. I used to keep wishing you would, but it seemed I was always the one to take the initiative."

He was right, Samantha thought. She had always waited for him to make the first move—not that she had ever had to wait long, for Max was all virile, passionate male. But perhaps she should have taken the initiative sometimes, should have shown him that she was more than just a willing partner, that she had needs and desires of her own.

"That's about to change," she said.

"Starting now?"

"Unless you have something else in mind," she teased.

"Are you kidding!"

Afterward, they would talk, she thought. She would tell him what she had learned from Edna, and would apologize for not having allowed him to explain. But for now, they had talked enough. This was a time for loving, for catching up on all the precious time they had lost.

A second later, Max was kissing her. His kisses were long and exploring. And she was exploring him, too, reveling in the wonderful feel and taste of his mouth.

When they drew apart to draw breath, she said, "Don't you think you're overdressed?"

He laughed softly and huskily. "Forgotten how to remedy that?"

"Want to bet?"

With those words, she went to work on his clothes. She began to undress him, slowly and seductively at first, button by button, heightening the suspense and driving them both a little crazy. But she was unable to maintain the slowness. As her impatience increased, and her fingers began to tremble, she pushed his shirt from his shoulders, letting it lie on the floor where it fell.

It was only when she came to the belt of his pants that she paused.

"You're not going to stop there?" She heard the amusement in his tone, but there was something else, too...a heightened eagerness and anticipation.

She looked up at him. "Max..."

"I'm not a stranger, darling. We've made love more times than both of us can count."

It made no sense at all that she should feel as if they were going to be making love for the first time. But there it was, she couldn't help feeling tremulous and vulnerable,

almost the way she had felt the very first time she had gone
to bed with Max.

"It's been so long," she whispered.

"Too long! Longer than any normal, warm-blooded male
can endure. It's been sheer hell sleeping in the same room
as you, afraid you'd bolt if I touched you."

"You slept like a baby," Samantha teased.

"Mean I actually had you fooled?" he asked wonder-
ingly. "I've been frustrated half out of my mind every
night. We're married, Samantha. And even if we weren't...
I've waited so long for you, my darling. Undress me.
Please!"

Her heart leaped every time he called her darling. At first
the endearment had made her angry, for she had been so
certain that it meant nothing to Max. Now it warmed her
and fanned her excitement. She was more deeply in love
with Max at this moment than she had ever been before.
When he called her his darling, it was as if he was inti-
mating they would have a future together, as if they would
be together always.

Suddenly it was easy to undress him. Max was right—
he wasn't a stranger. He was the man she had fallen in love
with five years earlier. She had never stopped loving him.
She never would.

When she had opened the belt buckle and loosened his
pants, Max stepped out of them, and held out his arms to
her.

She went to him eagerly, and as he lifted her from the
ground, she wound her arms around his neck. For a long
time they didn't move. Samantha, her feet dangling well
above the ground, exulted in the feeling of the muscular
body against hers. His arms were like steel around her, his
breath was warm against her face, and where her chest was
pressed against his, their hearts beat in unison.

Max groaned suddenly, and with Samantha still in his

arms, he moved toward the bed. Her arms remained around his neck as he put her down. And then he was lying beside her, two warm bodies, naked and throbbing and yearning to be one.

Their old pattern of lovemaking came back to them, and as they kissed and caressed and stirred each other to new heights of excitement, it was almost as if they had never been apart. And yet there was a difference. The last year had bred hunger and frustration, and now they brought to their lovemaking an intensity and a passion that was greater than anything they had ever experienced before.

They began to kiss once more: long, deep, searching kisses, a meeting of tongues and teeth and lips. They caressed each other, hands sliding over throats and backs and hips and thighs, fingers relearning shapes and textures which had once been so familiar. Max cupped Samantha's breasts in his hands, groaning with satisfaction as her nipples hardened in response to his touch. Samantha groaned in turn as his lips replaced his fingers, kissing, and nibbling lightly. Her blood was like fire in her veins, and the throbbing deep inside her was a kind of pain.

But they could only kiss and caress for so long. The moment came when they couldn't wait any longer. As Max entered her, Samantha gave a small moan of pleasure. Pleasure quickly turned to an explosion of ecstasy. *This* was what she had been deprived of for so long—this sensation of fireworks, this rapturous union of two loving bodies, straining together as if nothing could ever part them again.

Afterward, they lay for a while, still kissing and caressing, but more gently now, without quite the same urgency as had gripped them at the start.

"I love you," Max said after a while. "I've never, never stopped loving you, my darling."

Samantha turned to face him, her heart beating with a happiness she had never thought to know again. "I love you, too, Max. So much. So very much, darling.'' The endearment was like honey on her tongue.

''You're the most beautiful woman I've ever known. I don't think I'll ever get enough of you, Samantha.''

There was so much she wanted to say—that she would never get enough of him, either, that he would have to force her out of the house if he wanted to get rid of her—but Max had other things in mind besides talking. With his body covering hers, he began to kiss her again, and as she folded her arms around his waist, desire leaped inside her again, too. In no time, they were making love once more, with not quite the frenzy but all the joy of the first time.

They must have fallen asleep in each other's arms, for Samantha woke at some point to find Max's arms still around her, his breathing slow and steady against her breast. For a long time she lay there, enjoying the feel of the muscled body against her own, and caressing him softly so that he would not wake. She wished the night would never end so that they could lie like this always. And then she remembered the wonderful things he had said to her, the things they had said to each other, and she knew it didn't matter that the morning would come, because they would be spending the rest of their lives together.

She thought of Edna, and the things that woman had told her. She hadn't had a chance yet to tell Max what she had learned, but that didn't matter, either. They would talk in the morning, before he went to work.

She must have slept again, because the next time she awoke the sun was slanting in through the windows, and in the distance she could hear Annie talking to Melissa. Annie! Time to get her ready and off to kindergarten. Time for work, too. It was much later than she had realized.

Stretching luxuriously, Samantha reached her arm across the bed, only to find it empty. Max must have left already. For a moment she wondered if she had only dreamed that they had made love. Then she realized that she was naked, and she knew that it had really happened. Hugging herself, she tried to remember the last time she had been quite so happy.

"Don't *you* look like the cat that swallowed the cream."

"It's such a wonderful day, Melissa!" Samantha exclaimed exuberantly. "How can I help but be happy?"

"You haven't looked like this since I've been here. Neither has Max. Come to think of it, when I saw him earlier, he also looked as if he'd been at the cream."

Samantha felt her cheeks reddening. "He did?"

"Couldn't be a coincidence, could it?"

Samantha smiled at her sister-in-law. Their relationship had changed in the past week. Partly, Samantha thought, Annie had created a bond between them. Melissa adored the little girl, and Annie was beginning to reciprocate her feelings. Partly, too, Melissa seemed to understand at last that she couldn't control Max's life: for the first time, she actually seemed to accept Samantha as a member of the family.

Samantha, in turn, was beginning to grow quite fond of Max's sister. Acerbic Melissa might be, but she was also well-intentioned, and Samantha wished the two of them could have got off to a better start five years earlier. Perhaps things would have been different if she hadn't let herself be so intimidated by Melissa, but it wasn't too late for them to become friends now.

"Coincidence?" she repeated. "I guess not."

"You and Max are really putting it together again?"

"I think so."

Melissa's eyes searched her face. "You're still in love with him?"

In the past, this conversation could not have taken place. Now Samantha felt able to say, "Yes."

"When I came here," Melissa said thoughtfully, "I could have sworn there was no love lost between the two of you. I was amazed to find you were actually sharing a room. I mean, you'd been apart for almost a year, I was sure you hated each other."

"Sometimes things change," Samantha said softly.

"Are you going to tell me what caused the change?"

"I'd rather not…"

"I'm sorry, I shouldn't have asked. All I know is, you're both starry-eyed today."

Samantha laughed. It wasn't like her husband to wear his heart on his sleeve. "Max starry-eyed?" she said happily. "I wonder what he'd say to that description."

"More to the point," Melissa said slowly, "I wonder what he thinks of Dad's will now."

"You didn't think much of it," Samantha reminded her.

"I must admit, at the time I thought it was ridiculous. My father believing he could save a marriage from the grave."

"And now?" Samantha asked curiously, amazed that a week could have made such a difference in Melissa's attitude.

"I've changed my mind. Perhaps my earlier thinking was influenced by my own divorce. Nothing in the world could have saved my marriage. But as far as you and Max are concerned—Dad was right. His will was a stroke of genius."

"It was," Samantha agreed. "Not that I thought so when Max first told me about it. I was very upset at the time."

"Dad knew what he was doing. The condition relating to Annie's inheritance brought you back here for six months. And splitting Max's inheritance, putting a condition on the second half of it—that was smart, too. Gave Max the incentive to find a way of saving the marriage permanently."

Absorbed in her thoughts, Melissa was unaware that Samantha had turned ashen.

"What was that about Max?" Samantha felt as if she had been punched very hard in the stomach. She felt the blood draining from her cheeks, and her throat was so dry suddenly that it was an effort to get the words out.

Melissa looked at her, and was shocked in turn. "Oh my God!"

"What was that you said about Max?"

"It wasn't important." Melissa was genuinely shaken.

Not important? Didn't her sister-in-law understand that she had just turned Samantha's world upside down?

"Please!" Samantha said urgently. "You can't put me off now. What was that about Max and the inheritance?"

"Nothing." Visibly agitated, Melissa was about to walk away.

Samantha caught her arm. "You have to tell me! You've said this much, you can't leave me hanging now. *What about Max?*"

"I wish I hadn't said anything." Melissa was trembling as she tried to pull away from Samantha. "I thought you knew. I was so certain you knew."

"No."

"Well, I can't tell you anything. Whatever you want to know, you'll have to ask Max."

"Just tell me one thing—are Max and Annie subject to the same conditions?"

"Not exactly. Don't ask me more, Samantha. You're putting me in a terrible position."

"You brought it up, Melissa."

"I know, and it's my fault. But I didn't mean to... Oh God, Max will be furious! I don't want to say more, Samantha. I can't."

But Samantha had heard enough anyway. "Max receives his inheritance in two parts. One part goes to him automatically. The other is conditional on us putting our marriage together again.'' She looked at Melissa. "That's it, isn't it?''

Melissa's lips were pressed together tightly, it was clear she didn't intend to say another word. She didn't have to. Samantha had all the answers she needed.

It was late afternoon when Samantha found the message on the answering machine. Grimly she listened to it. "Meet me at the marina at eight. I'm sure either Melissa or Helen will look after Annie.''

So Max thought she would go sailing with him. The sheer nerve of the man! Oh, but he had gone about things so cleverly. He hadn't had to try very hard to make her fall in love with him again. She had never stopped loving him, and Max, clever Max, had known that. But to think he would stoop so low as to con her into going back to him permanently just so that he could get his inheritance, that was unforgivable.

Briefly she thought of Edna. True, she now knew that Max hadn't slept with the woman the night she had caught them together. But that had nothing to do with the terms of William's will. Max should have been honest with her— *he'd owed her that much*. The fact that he had kept the truth from her made his motives suspect.

Lips tight, she dialed his private line. His secretary answered the phone. Max had been out most of the day, she said. He had already checked his messages a few times. No, she didn't think he would be in contact with her again that afternoon.

Now what? Samantha wondered. She could let him hang around the marina, wondering when she was going to arrive. Wouldn't he just love being stood up! The sought-after Max Anderson, left in the lurch by the woman he was certain he had charmed—and duped. It would be no more than he deserved.

However, on further reflection, Samantha thought she might as well go and meet him. It was one way of avoiding unpleasantness at the house, where Annie or Melissa or Helen might overhear them. The water, away from everyone else, was the perfect place for this final argument.

Changing into tight-fitting jeans and a scarlet T-shirt, she left her bedroom and hurried down the stairs. Melissa had said she would look after Annie. Her sister-in-law eyed her anxiously as she went to the door.

"Samantha..." she began, her expression still ridden with guilt.

Samantha touched her arm. Melissa wasn't to blame because Max had deceived her. "It's okay," she said quietly. "Whatever happens now, it won't be your fault."

When she drove into the car park of the marina, she saw Max's car. He was nowhere in sight, so Samantha walked to the place where the boat was always berthed. Max had bought the boat soon after their wedding. Ironically they had called it *The Sammax,* as if they had just assumed that Samantha and Max would always be a unit.

More than a year had passed since Samantha had been to the marina, but she spotted the boat immediately. Max was swabbing the deck with a long-handled mop. His back was to Samantha, so that he was unaware of her presence.

It was on the tip of her tongue to call out to him, but something stopped her. In shorts and a tank top, he looked more like a sailor than the lawyer who had so recently triumphed in court. His arms and legs were deeply tanned, long and hard and rippling with muscles, and his dark hair was ruffled by the slight wind. Even now, when he was working, there was that sexuality that was always with him.

Samantha swallowed hard as she watched him. In some

irrational part of her, she wished Melissa hadn't told her about William's will. How differently this day would be turning out, if she didn't know the truth.

Max turned around suddenly. "Samantha!" he called gladly. Putting down the mop, he ran to the side of the boat and held out a hand to her. There was nothing she could do at that moment except let him help her on to the deck. After the previous night, it would seem strange if she didn't, and there was no sense in alerting his suspicions before she was ready to.

"Hi, gorgeous." He smiled down at her, before kissing her.

Samantha's senses leaped, those treacherous senses that betrayed her every time. She didn't want to react to Max, not after his dishonesty. But there was something inside her that she could not control, that flicker of response that sprang to life in the very core of her being; she could not help responding to Max's smile, to the sparkle in the dark eyes, to his vital sexuality.

"You look lovely," he said warmly.

"Thanks," she said stiffly.

Max shot her a puzzled look. "Glad you got my message. I wasn't sure if you'd be here."

"Are you ever unsure of anything, Max?"

"Is that supposed to mean something, darling?" He went on before she could answer. "The Tweedle Brothers gave you a rough time at work?"

"The *Tweedle Brothers* never give me a rough time," she replied, wondering if he registered the emphasis.

"You seem a bit tense all the same. We'll go out on the water, and I hope you'll relax." His eyes sparkled again. "And I have other plans for us, too—after we get home tonight."

His meaning was so unmistakable that Samantha felt her

muscles tighten. Some of her happiest memories were of
times spent on this boat. If only she could have enjoyed
sailing with Max now. But she had to be realistic. Max—
handsome, *devious* Max—was a sexy con-man. So certain
of himself that it had never occurred to him that Samantha
would come to see through his game.

"Plans?" she asked lightly.

"Eye-popping ones." His grin was wicked.

"Want to hear about them?"

Samantha felt anger battle with desire, with desire threat-
ening to win the upper hand. It was the anger she had to
hold on to, she reminded herself. She could not give in to
the part of her that was dying to hear what Max had in
mind for them.

She was here for one reason only, and the sooner she
told Max exactly what she knew and what she thought of
him, the better. But she had to choose the right moment,
and this wasn't it.

She was relieved when he left her side and prepared to
detach the boat from its moorings. Here and there people
called out friendly greetings, and Samantha called back to
them. This was all so familiar. It was also heart-
wrenchingly painful, because she knew she would never
come here again.

Max was an excellent sailor. With an expertise that came
from years on boats, he navigated *The Sammax* through the
maze of moored vessels. Samantha leaned against the railing, watching the water rather than the superb figure she
couldn't stop loving, even though she wanted to.

It was early evening, a time of day she had always loved.
The sky was cloudless, and the breeze that blew over the
ocean crested the waves with white. The Sound was
crowded with boats of all description, all filled, it seemed
to Samantha, with people who didn't have a care in the

world beyond enjoying themselves. She wondered if she was the only one with a heart that felt as if it would break.

She stiffened when Max called her name.

"Yes...?"

"Come and stand with me, darling."

"Actually I'm quite happy here at the railing."

"Trust me to steer wherever I like?"

There was a time when Samantha would have trusted Max with her life! Yet now, looking at the dark eyes in the dynamic face, she knew she couldn't trust him at all. The knowledge intensified her pain.

She shrugged. "Sure, why not?"

"I could decide to sail away to the ends of the earth with you." The words were teasing, but she was aware that he was looking at her curiously.

"The ends of the earth?" Samantha asked lightly. "Oh, I don't think so, Max. I don't think you'd be happy anywhere but here in New York. I think you like to be where there's big business and lots of money. Not to mention intrigue."

The curious look intensified. "I'd be happy anywhere as long as I was with you. You and Annie. Don't you know that, darling?"

Liar, she thought, and decided to let him get away with the meaningless endearment—at least for now. Aloud she said, "You know all the right things to say to a girl, Max."

"You make it sound as if I don't mean them."

Samantha gave a small, hard laugh. "Gee, Max, why on earth would you think that?"

"I have no idea," he said mildly. "I do know you're in a strange mood today. Why don't you stop talking nonsense, and come and join me here at the wheel?"

After a moment she went to him, trying not to stiffen when he put his arm around her. Her precious husband was clearly playing his nasty little game to the hilt. Well, let him enjoy himself a while longer, let him kid himself into believing that she was deceived by him. When he found out that she was on to his wiles, his dismay would be all the sweeter to witness.

"What's wrong?" he asked.

"Wrong, Max?"

His arm tightened around her, and he leaned his cheek on her head. Having decided to postpone the moment of truth, Samantha let him do it. Max was clever enough to talk his way out of any situation—even this one. It would be foolish to give him the advantage of time in which to plan what he could say. Far better to let him believe she was still the naive girl he had swept off her feet five years earlier, dazzling her with his lavish attention, so that she was willing to believe anything he told her.

"There *is* something," he insisted. He caressed her arm, and she had to force herself not to feel anything.

"You keep saying that," she muttered.

"I know you, Samantha. You're not the same person you were yesterday."

The words got to her, so that she spoke without thinking. "*Yesterday!* Yesterday was before I—" Horrified at what she had been so close to saying, she bit down hard on her lower lip.

Max lifted his head. "Before what?" He was watching her intently.

"Forget I said that!"

"No. If something's wrong, I want to know about it."

Samantha shook her head. He would know soon enough, but not yet. The timing was all wrong. Besides, it would do Max good to endure a bit of suspense.

"I want to know everything about you, Samantha. The good things as well as the bad. If something's worrying you, I want to share it with you. That's what marriage is all about, darling.''

Well, wasn't he a fine one to talk about marriage! He looked and sounded genuinely concerned. If she didn't know better, she would actually be touched. Seething with anger, Samantha moved her feet restlessly on the wet deck. Max was being the perfect husband, playing his part so superbly that she was torn between wanting to believe him and knowing she couldn't.

"What do you think marriage is about, Max?" It wasn't the question she had intended asking, but she asked it anyway.

"That's easy," he responded. "Marriage is love and sharing. Concern for each other. Wanting only the best for the most important person in your life."

"How about trust?"

Max stiffened, as if he realized she was setting a trap for him. "Trust? Trust is basic, without it there's nothing." He paused a moment. "If this is about it Edna, I wish you'd drop it—or finally let me explain."

Samantha looked up at him. "This has nothing to do with Edna."

"Well!" He seemed surprised. "That's a change. I'm glad, because I have things I want to say tonight, and they don't concern Edna." He drew her toward him again. "Whatever's bothering you, darling, can't you relax for a while?"

Beneath their feet, the boat rocked and swayed with the swell of the tide. For a while there was only sensation: the sensuousness of their legs brushing together, the beat of Max's heart in rhythm with her own, the curve of his throat around her head.

It was a constant source of amazement to Samantha that her mind could ask one thing of her, her body another. It wasn't that she had forgotten how angry she was with

Max—*not for a moment could she forget that*—but the physical contact with him wrought its usual magic. A magic that was almost impossible to fight, no matter how hard she tried.

Perhaps she shouldn't have closed her eyes, or surrendered herself to the intimacy of the moment, but she did so anyway. It was the last time she would have Max's arm around her. She loved him, she had always loved him. For some reason, it was possible for a woman to be terribly angry with a man, and yet love him anyway. That being the case, these last moments of togetherness were a kind of present to herself.

Now, she thought, as he lifted his head and removed his arm from her shoulder. No sense in postponing what she had to say any longer.

She was about to speak, when Max said, "Hold the wheel, will you?"

She did as he asked, and saw him go to the cabin. The moment of telling had passed, but only temporarily. She would still find the right time to say what she had to.

Max was back minutes later, carrying a bottle of wine and two glasses. Samantha tensed as he began to pour the wine. This was something she hadn't counted on. But it didn't matter, she would still find her moment to talk.

He handed her a glass before taking back the wheel with his free hand.

"A toast," he said softly.

"Another one?" The look in his eyes made it difficult for her to keep her voice from shaking. "Melissa made a toast yesterday."

"That was to winning the case." His eyes held hers in a way that unnerved her. "This one is for you, darling."

The way he spoke, so softly and intimately, made what she had to say much more difficult. But she had to say it nevertheless. The sooner the better. She couldn't postpone it any longer.

"Max—" she began urgently.

But he went on, as if he hadn't heard her. "To you, Samantha. My precious wife."

"Max!"

"Wait, darling, let me finish. There's more. Let's also drink to both of us. And to our marriage."

Oh, but he was rotten. More unscrupulous than she could ever have imagined. Playing on her emotions, on her love for him, so that he could get what he wanted.

She looked at him cynically. "Our marriage?"

"Our marriage, my darling—which is going to last forever this time." His eyes were steady, loving and clear.

"Forever?" Samantha repeated.

"Forever." He clinked his glass against hers. When he had taken a sip, he said, "You're not drinking, Samantha."

She glanced down at the glass she'd forgotten she was holding. "I'm not thirsty."

"You're not even going to drink to the toasts?"

"I don't think so, Max."

He looked down at her from his great height, his eyes thoughtful.

And then, to her astonishment, he gave her a small gift-wrapped package.

"This is a repetition of yesterday," she said slowly. "I gave you the tiepin."

"Today it's my turn. Open it, Samantha."

Deep inside Samantha, a trembling had started. It was a moment before she found her voice. "What if I don't want it?"

He took the wineglass from her hand. "How can you know? You haven't looked at it yet."

"I don't have to."

"Open it, darling."

Yielding to Max's insistence, Samantha slowly took off the gift paper. Her trembling increased when she saw a small box. She had no wish to open it, but again Max insisted.

And then she was staring in shock at the most beautiful ring she had ever seen: a lovely pear-shaped diamond embedded in a wide gold band that was encrusted with smaller diamonds.

The boat was running a steady course now, so that Max didn't have to steer. He took her left hand. "Let me put it on for you, darling." His voice was husky.

"No…"

"Yes, my dearest love. Do you realize what this is, darling? It's a second wedding ring. Given to you with all my love. For the marriage that is going to last us all the rest of our lives."

He was beginning to slip the ring on to her finger, when Samantha recoiled. She had the satisfaction of seeing Max flinch.

"Louse!" she hissed.

"*What?*"

"I never dreamed you could sink so low."

It was Max's turn to look shocked. "What on earth are you talking about?"

Thrusting the ring back at him, she said bitterly, "Did you really think I would wear this?"

"I hoped you'd be happy to," he said tightly.

"How could you, Max? This ring is an insult."

"An *insult?*" He was stunned.

"Worse than that. It's a travesty."

"If you're talking about Edna—" he began.

"This has nothing to do with Edna!"

"What then?" He actually had the gall to look puzzled.

"I can't believe you'd talk about a marriage that will last forever. As for a second wedding ring—" Samantha's voice was heavy with scorn "—if that isn't a joke!"

"A joke?" Max's eyes had narrowed. "After last night?"

"Last night, yes." Samantha clasped her hands tightly, so that Max wouldn't see they were shaking. "You must have thought me an idiot last night! The great seduction scene. Did you find it difficult not to laugh?"

"I don't know what you're talking about." His expression had changed. When the boat had left the marina, his face had been alive with zest and vitality, laughter settling easily around his eyes. Now his face had turned hard.

"Don't you, Max? Don't you really? Remember, it's me you're talking to now, not a jury. Your act doesn't impress me."

"Have you gone completely crazy, Samantha?"

"On the contrary—I've come to my senses. I just wish it had happened sooner."

He looked so puzzled that Samantha allowed herself a moment of satisfaction. Oh, but it was good to see Max, her beloved Max, at a disadvantage for once.

At last he said, "Mind telling me what last night was all about? That sexy nightie. The invitation to make love. I thought—I hoped—your feelings for me had changed. Your feelings about our marriage. Was I so wrong?"

Samantha took her time about answering. It would be easy to give Max a flippant answer, but since this was the last serious conversation they would ever have, she felt the need to be honest with him.

"You weren't wrong."

His head went up. "You did change your mind about our marriage?"

"I thought I did."

"*Samantha,*" he exclaimed, taking a step toward her. "Then that does mean there's hope!"

"Hope?" She moved away from him. "For our so-called marriage? Forget it!"

Beneath Max's tan, his face seemed to pale. "Is this some game you're playing?" he asked harshly. "Because if it is, I don't think much of it."

"Game?" Samantha gave a painful laugh.

Dimly she remembered Edna saying something similar, only the context had been different. Yesterday's confrontation, the happiness she had felt by the end of it, seemed to have taken place in another time. So much had happened since then.

"Mind telling me what the hell you're talking about?"

"This game we've been playing. Till now, you've been making all the rules and expecting me to follow them blindly. And I did follow them, didn't I? Stupid, gullible Samantha. But the game has changed, Max."

"It has?" He was eyeing her warily.

"Yes." She threw him a tart look. "You see, there were rules I didn't know about until today."

"Such as?"

"Such as the other condition in your father's will. The one that made the second half of your inheritance conditional on whether our marriage went on."

Something flickered momentarily in the dark eyes, then was gone. A muscle moved below the strong line of the jaw. "So that's what this is all about." His voice was taut.

She had been wrong about Edna. Maybe she was wrong again now. Maybe Melissa had got her facts mixed up...maybe she hadn't known what she was talking about. With all her heart, Samantha hoped Melissa was wrong.

She was barely breathing as she waited for Max to deny the accusation. But Max didn't deny it. Evidently the terrible thing his sister had told her was the truth.

"Why didn't you tell me, Max? I shouldn't have found out from someone else."

"From whom?"

She had no wish to make trouble for Melissa. "It doesn't matter."

"Stan Manson? No—he wouldn't have told you."

"I told you, it doesn't matter."

"*Melissa* told you?"

"Don't blame her, Max. She wasn't trying to cause a problem. She thought I knew."

After a long silence, Max said, "And now that you do— it shouldn't make a difference."

Samantha stared at him incredulously. "It makes all the difference in the world!"

Max pushed a hand through his hair, his expression distraught. "I can see you're shocked, but—"

"Shock doesn't begin to describe what I feel! I feel betrayed! Cheap and used and exploited."

Max reached for her hand, but she pulled it back fiercely. "Don't touch me!"

"I haven't betrayed you, Samantha. Listen to me, darling—"

"Never again, Max. I'll never listen to you again."

"You have to." His eyes were wild. "Nothing has changed, no matter what you think. I want our marriage to continue. For its own sake. Take the ring, darling. Please."

It was warm on the water, but Samantha felt cold. "You don't get it, do you, Max? It's over."

"I don't accept that! Our marriage has nothing to do with the inheritance."

"It has everything to do with it! I have to know one

thing, Max. Why didn't you tell me? Because you knew I wouldn't agree to come back?''

"Samantha—"

"It was one thing to make an effort for Annie's sake—how could I say no to that? But if I'd known you also stood to gain from my return, well, maybe I'd have had second thoughts. I'm not saying I would have, but it was possible, wasn't it?''

"It was possible," Max admitted, his eyes bleak. "Samantha…I had such hopes for tonight. The start of a whole new future for us. It's not too late, darling.''

Samantha felt sick as she listened to him speak. "A future based on deception," she said bitterly.

"No, darling," Max said, his tone urgent. "We can make it work. I know we can.''

She shook her head. "It's too late. We both know it.''

"How can I make you believe me? I wish now that I'd told you the truth, but I didn't know how you'd react. Samantha, darling, my inheritance has nothing to do with my feelings for you. I love you, don't you understand?''

She shook her head.

For a while they were both silent. The boat bobbed playfully, moving up and down with the waves. A seagull swooped down, perching a few seconds on the railing before flying away again.

"What happens now?" Max asked.

"I'll stay the six months—for Annie's sake. Then I'll go.''

"Samantha…"

"I don't want to talk about it again, Max. I can't.''

ROSEMARY CARTER 171

[...] ing. Max. Why don't you tell me? Because you know I wouldn't agree to come back."
"Samantha—"
"It was one thing to make an effort for Annie's sake. How could I do so now—knowing that you are [...] to go back on the agreement—"

[...]

CHAPTER TEN

SAMANTHA and Annie returned to Manhattan on the day the six months were up.

When Max understood that Samantha wanted nothing more to do with him, and that their relationship couldn't be salvaged, he tried to find a way of getting around the conditions of his father's will. He and Stan Manson put their heads together, and tried to find a loophole that would not jeopardize Annie's inheritance. But in the end, Samantha had to stay on Long Island the full six months.

Not that Max didn't try to patch things up between Samantha and himself, but she would have none of it. Knowing that his financial future depended on keeping his marriage going, she could not trust his protestations of love, no matter how sincere they sounded.

In Annie's presence, the two parents maintained an amicable front. They both knew they couldn't involve the little girl in their own unhappy situation. Away from the child, however, there was an icy silence between them.

Samantha never again accused Max of betraying her. She had said all she had to—there was no point in bringing it up again. She moved through her days like an automaton, glad to have her job to go to in the mornings, and spending every afternoon with Annie. The evenings developed their own kind of routine: sometimes Max didn't come home for dinner, and even when he did, he went out again soon afterward.

He didn't even wait for Melissa to leave, but moved his possessions out of the master bedroom and into the den. His sister was heart-sore at the trouble she had caused, blaming herself for telling Samantha about the condition attached to Max's inheritance. A tight-lipped Samantha assured her that she wasn't at fault. On the contrary, she was glad she had learned the truth before the relationship could go any further.

Samantha kept wondering whether Max was seeing Edna. Now that her own relationship with him had finally ended, there would be a void in his life, and he might be happy to have it filled by a willing and available Edna. Samantha told herself she didn't care.

She told nobody how lonely she felt in the master bedroom. The emptiness in her bed was a kind of torment, and many was the night that she cried herself to sleep. Now and then she wondered what would happen if Max came to her bed and tried to make love to her. She could only hope that she would have the strength to resist him. Giving in to him would be the final blow to her self-esteem.

But Max did not appear.

The divorce action that had been put on hold when she returned to him would go on again now. It wouldn't be long before the final papers were granted. Then it would be time for her to move on with her own life, a life that was unlikely to include another man. Samantha could not begin to imagine falling in love again.

Annie cried bitterly when the time came to leave, the tears streaming down her face in rivulets of sorrow. Melissa had left the house months ago, but Helen hugged her tightly, her own eyes full of tears. Max was not there when they left. He had said his goodbyes before he left for work that morning. Samantha suspected that he didn't know if he could handle the emotion.

She couldn't help feeling like a criminal as she drove away, with Annie weeping on the back seat. Once, involuntarily, she glanced into her rearview mirror, and saw the lovely house with Helen still standing on the steps, and waving madly. Until this minute, Samantha had managed to keep a tight rein on her emotions—at least outwardly—but now the tears ran down her face as well.

When the lump that filled her throat had cleared somewhat, she tried to talk to Annie, but the little girl would not answer her. A grief-stricken Samantha could not blame her. It made sense that Annie would think her mother was dragging her away from her father and the home that she loved. Samantha could only hope that the day would come when her daughter would understand what had happened. But that day was years away.

They returned to an apartment that seemed musty and unlived-in, even though Betty, a friendly neighbor, had watered the plants and opened the windows occasionally. After the beautiful Long Island house, so airy and spacious, the apartment seemed a little depressing.

"What shall we do today, Annie?" Samantha asked when she had flung open the windows and emptied the suitcases. "Feel like going to the park?" And when the little girl didn't answer, "How about going for an ice cream?"

Annie shook her head mournfully. "I just want to go back to Daddy and Helen."

Samantha felt as if her heart would break. Kneeling, she put her arms around the child. "I know, honey. I know how sad you are, and I'm sad, too. But this is the way it has to be, Annie."

"Doesn't Daddy love me anymore?"

"He loves you very much, honey. More than I can ever tell you. Leaving him has nothing to do with the way he feels about you. It's a grown-up thing, and doesn't concern you. Annie, honey, you're going to see lots of Daddy, I promise."

Annie looked only slightly consoled. Samantha, who had left her own heart behind her with Max, wondered how long it would take them both to settle down again emotionally.

Within a week they had got back into their old routine. Annie went back to kindergarten, and Samantha to her job. When Brian heard they had returned, he phoned and invited Samantha to go out with him. Gently she refused him.

Seeing Brian again would be a terrible mistake. She would not see any man until she was certain she had got over Max—if that ever happened. The last thing Samantha wanted was to enter another relationship on the rebound.

"There's someone else," Brian said.

"No."

"It's still Max?"

"Please... I can't talk about Max," Samantha said.

"Don't tell me you're still in love with the guy." He sounded disgusted.

Samantha wished Brian was a little more sensitive. "I didn't say that," she said quietly. "But I'm not comfortable going out with anybody else. Not yet, Brian. I'm sorry."

Max arrived that weekend to see Annie. As Samantha opened the door to him, she made a great effort to keep her face expressionless. All week she had been dreading this visit, and seeing Max again was every bit as hard as she'd thought it would be. She could only pray that the pain of missing him would grow less with time.

"Are you all right?" he asked, when Annie left the room for a moment to fetch a sweater.

"Great."

His eyes searched her face. "Would you tell me if you weren't?"

"Sure," she said, and knew that he was aware of both lies.

She missed him. Constantly. Agonizingly. With such anguish that it felt sometimes as if a dagger pierced her heart. The nights were the worst time. Often in the mornings,

Samantha got out of bed feeling exhausted because she had spent so many hours without sleeping.

They had been back in Manhattan a month, when Samantha's boss called her into his office. With some embarrassment, he told her that the company was going through a bad time financially. He had no option but to lay off several members of staff, and Samantha was one of them. He hoped things would improve quickly, and that new orders would come in. Everybody would be rehired when that happened; maybe as soon as a month.

"Come to us," said her sister, Dorothy, the moment she heard the news. "It's ages since Arthur and I last saw you and Annie. I've *missed* you so much."

"I don't know... It means taking Annie out of kindergarten. And I should be looking for other work until things pick up again at the company."

"Don't be silly." Dorothy was succinct as always. "There's no earthly reason for you to hang around New York for a month. We'll be traveling up the Pacific Coast all the way to Oregon, and you and Annie will come with us. It's a wonderful drive, Sam, and you need a holiday. Please, Samantha, say you'll come."

Samantha couldn't help laughing. "How could anyone say no to such eloquence? Okay, sis, I'll come. And thank you."

Max was not happy with the news. He would miss his visits with Annie, but he didn't put any obstacles in Samantha's way. "Call me regularly, Samantha. I'll want to know where you are, and that you're okay."

"You'll want to hear about Annie, and I know she'll want to talk to you. I'll make certain she calls you every few days."

Max must have registered the rebuff, because he was silent for a second. In a new voice, he said, "What should I do about your mail? Where should I send it?"

"Hmm..." Samantha thought for a moment. "Why don't you just send it to the apartment? Betty will be in every few days to check up on things, and I can arrange for her to keep the mail."

"Sure that's what you want? If you tell me where you'll be, I can send you whatever comes here to the house."

That would mean regular contact with Max. Speaking to him herself, instead of just dialing his number and putting Annie on the line.

"On second thought," she said, "I'll ask Betty to forward the lot to me. There'll be the mail that goes to you, as well as anything that comes to the apartment. I'll always know a few days beforehand where we'll be, and I'll make sure Betty has the address."

"Will she do it?"

"I'm sure she will. I've helped her when she's been away. We have a kind of reciprocal agreement."

"Samantha..."

His voice was warm and vital. Closing her eyes, Samantha could picture him sitting in the den, with his chair turned to the window so that he could see over the water. Suddenly she was swept with a fierce pain of longing.

Gripping the receiver tightly, she said, "Yes?"

"Let me give you some money."

"No, thanks, Max."

"I know how independent you are, but to tide you over at least. If you feel so strongly about it, you can pay me back when you start working again."

"No, Max."

"Samantha—"

"Thanks for offering," she said firmly, " but I don't want your money." Then she put down the phone.

They were in San Francisco a week later. Dorothy and Arthur were wildlife photographers, a childless couple who adored Annie, and made a huge fuss over her. As for Samantha, the moment she saw her sister again, she was glad she had made the decision to leave New York. When she saw Dorothy running toward her at the airport, her eyes filled with unexpected tears.

"I'm sorry, I don't know what's come over me," she murmured helplessly.

"I do," Dorothy said when she had hugged them both. "You've had a lot to put up with, and you've been strong for too long." She hugged them again. "It's so *good* to see you both."

Two days later, Arthur packed the camper, and the four of them left San Francisco.

For Samantha the holiday began the moment they left the city. Arthur and Dorothy seemed to know all the by-ways on the route up the coastline. They explored quaint villages, always finding a place where Annie could have an ice cream, or a lollipop that was nearly the size of her face. They went to farms where they picked fruit, and to the Napa Valley where the adults tasted wine. And everywhere there were beaches, rugged yet beautiful, with craggy cliffs and huge rollers. Dorothy and Samantha would find a rock to sit on, while Arthur would run along the sand with Annie, collecting shells as they went.

"He's wonderful with her," Samantha said, at least once every day.

"He's a good guy," Dorothy agreed.

"I'm so glad you persuaded me to come. Annie is having a wonderful holiday. We both are."

What Samantha didn't tell her sister was that Annie often cried herself to sleep at night. As much as she was enjoying the holiday and all the attention her uncle and aunt lavished on her, the little girl was missing her father. Every two or three days, Samantha would see to it that Annie spoke to Max, and afterward she was always a little upset.

As for Samantha, she was missing Max as much as ever. She had hoped the holiday would put an end to the emptiness she felt whenever she thought of him. The lovely days spent with her sister and Arthur were a wonderful distraction, but the emptiness was a constant that never disappeared.

They had been traveling a week when Samantha's first batch of mail arrived. She glanced through it quickly. There was a check from the Tweedle Brothers, together with an affectionate note; a postcard from Helen for Annie; a few official letters including one from Samantha's lawyer; and another card for Annie, this one from Max, hand-drawn and with a joke on it.

Nothing for Samantha from Max. She blinked back stupid tears. It was obvious Max wouldn't be writing to her. There was nothing left to say, at least nothing personal, now that their relationship had ended. Any correspondence relating to the divorce would be handled by their respective lawyers—and what else could there be?

Mail arrived regularly after that. Samantha would call Betty and tell her where to send it. Each time there was a postcard or a letter from Max to Annie. Not one personal word to Samantha.

The holiday came to an end at last. Dorothy begged Samantha to remain in San Francisco a while longer, but Samantha knew it was time for her to get on with her real life. A few days later, she and Annie flew back to New York.

This time the apartment looked more inviting. Expecting their arrival, Betty had opened the windows, dusted and even baked a cake. The two women had a cup of coffee together, and when Betty had heard all about their travels, Samantha thanked her for forwarding the mail.

"I sent you everything except the junk stuff," Betty said. "The fliers and brochures. Oh, and a newspaper—didn't think it was worth sending that, either. I knew you'd get all the news in California."

"Newspaper?" Samantha asked.

"Here it is." Betty picked up a large brown envelope from the kitchen counter.

Samantha glanced at it without much interest. One side of the envelope must have got torn in the mail, so that the contents were clearly visible: it was a newspaper, just as Betty had said. She couldn't imagine why anyone would have sent it to her, but it wasn't really important.

When Betty had gone, Samantha put a tired little girl to bed. She poured herself another couple of coffee, and sat down at the kitchen table to drink it. The brown envelope was still where she'd left it. Idly she picked it up and turned it over.

Her heart jumped as she recognized Max's handwriting. With fingers that were suddenly shaking, she opened the envelope and took out a copy of the *New York Times*.

Why had Max sent it?

Thoroughly puzzled, Samantha began to look through the paper. The breath stopped in her throat as she turned a page and saw two familiar faces—her father-in-law's and her own. A great trembling seized her as she began to read the article that accompanied the pictures.

Max Anderson, well-known New York lawyer, has set up The William And Samantha Anderson Scholarship Fund. Intended to finance the legal education of two deserving students every year, the scholarship has been founded in honor of two people Max Anderson loved—

his recently deceased father, and his wife, Samantha. The scholarship money is to come from an inheritance, which William Anderson had left to his son.

By the time Samantha reached the end of the article, her eyes were blurred with tears. For several minutes she sat quite still, unable to move, barely able to think. When her eyes had cleared, she looked at the date of the paper. Three weeks had gone by since it had been printed.

Hurriedly she picked up the phone and began to dial. She got halfway through the number before putting down the receiver. Still trembling, she walked to the window and looked outside. It didn't take her long to make a decision.

It was midmorning of the next day when Samantha drove up to the lovely Long Island house, with Annie shouting gleefully in the back seat.

"We're back, Mommy, we're back!"

"Yes, honey, we are." Samantha's throat was thick with unshed tears as she opened the back door of the car and took Annie's hand.

It was Saturday. Max was nowhere in sight, but Samantha saw his car in the garage. With Annie skipping excitedly beside her, she walked to the front door and rang the bell. Helen opened the door.

"Samantha!" she exclaimed joyfully. "And Annie." She bent to give Annie a hug. "I'm so happy to see you."

When Samantha had said hello, she asked quietly, "Max—is he here?"

Helen nodded in the direction of the boat dock at the bottom of the garden. Then she took Annie's hand, and said, "Come and see what I have for you, pet."

Samantha walked away alone, down a winding path bordered with roses. She saw Max long before she reached the dock. He was sitting on an old wooden bench, his shoulders hunched forward, his chin leaning on his hands. He wasn't looking out over the water as he so often did. Instead he seemed to have withdrawn inside himself, as if he had retreated to a world where nobody could reach him. Samantha thought she had never seen him look quite so vulnerable and disconsolate, and she felt her heart wrench inside her.

He did not hear her come. She stopped beside him, touched his shoulder and said softly, "Max."

For a moment he didn't move, and then his head jerked upward, and he stared at Samantha, almost as if he didn't believe she was real.

"Max..."

"Samantha," he said, his voice hoarse and broken. "Oh God, Samantha, I thought you'd never come."

"I'm here." Her throat was so dry that she could hardly speak. "And Annie's here, too. She's with Helen."

His appearance shocked her; she found it hard to believe that he could have changed so much in such a short time. His face was haggard, as if he hadn't slept for months, and his eyes had a wild look.

"I saw the paper," Samantha said shakily. "Read about the scholarship."

"I kept hoping you'd contact me. When the weeks passed and I didn't hear from you, I thought it really was all over between us."

"I didn't see the paper till yesterday. Betty didn't forward it to me."

Max looked thunderstruck. *"She didn't?"*

"She realized it was a newspaper, and didn't think I'd need it."

"And all this time I thought..."

Samantha knelt by his feet and put her arms around his waist. "What did you think, Max?"

"That it was all over. That there was no hope. That you really did hate me."

Samantha sat forward on her heels, and rested her head on Max's lap. She was quite still as he stroked her hair, tentatively at first, and then more firmly.

A minute or two passed before she lifted her head. "I've never hated you, Max. Even when I was angry. Even when I still believed you'd been having an affair with Edna. Despite everything, I never stopped loving you."

"Samantha!" he groaned. "I can't believe I'm hearing this."

"It's true, my darling."

He took her hands from his waist and sat upright, so that he could look into her face. "Am I dreaming, or did you really speak about Edna in the past tense?"

"I did," she said, and then she proceeded to tell him how she had confronted the woman, and what she had learned.

"Why didn't you tell me?" Max demanded. "I kept trying to explain to you about Edna, and you were never willing to listen. When you found out the truth, why didn't you tell me?"

"I was going to, Max. *After* I had finished seducing you. I had it all planned."

"Ah, the grand seduction." He grinned wickedly, and for the first time Samantha saw a return of the old Max. "A night I'll never forget." He paused, then said, "Why didn't you tell me afterward?"

"I meant to, but we fell asleep. And the next day…"

He finished the sentence for her. "You heard about the other condition in Dad's will."

"Yes."

"Melissa still hasn't forgiven herself for telling you. She

likes you, Samantha—did you know? It just took her a long time to realize it. And now she's hoping it isn't too late for us.''

"It isn't too late, my darling." Samantha leaned against Max once more. Happiness was springing to life inside her, and this time she knew she could trust her feelings.

She only lifted her head again when Max said, "Don't you want to know about the scholarship?"

"You've really given your inheritance away?"

"I always intended to. I have enough money without what Dad left me. Enough for you and me and Annie. The scholarship was always meant to be in your honor as well as a memorial to my father. There's so much you don't know, darling."

"Tell me," she said urgently.

"After you left me the first time, I was desperate to get you back. You wouldn't let me tell you about Edna, and so I had to find another way. Dad was as devastated as I was about the whole thing. We both knew he was desperately ill—and we discussed putting the condition in the will, the one dealing with Annie's inheritance."

"So you knew about it all along?" Samantha whispered.

"Actually," Max admitted, "it was my idea. I mentioned it to Dad, and he was eager to go along with it. We both agreed that if anything would bring you back, it would be Annie's interests. We also decided on the six-month period. I had a feeling you might not want to stay longer than that. Somehow I had to woo you back in that time."

"And the other condition, Max? The one relating to your inheritance?"

"That was Dad's doing. I knew nothing about it until after he died. He must have thought that splitting my inheritance would give me an additional incentive to work on our marriage. As if that was necessary! I already had the incentive I needed—to win back the only woman I've ever loved.''

"But you didn't tell me, Max."

"How could I? You'd made it so clear that you were just coming back for Annie's sake. If you'd thought I stood to gain myself, you might have refused. I couldn't take the chance, darling. I knew I had to wait till the scholarship was officially set up, till I could prove to you that I wouldn't be gaining financially from your return.''

"This is all so incredible," Samantha murmured. "Max... Darling... What would have happened if I hadn't seen the article? If I hadn't come back today?''

"I would have gone to you. I've spent the last two hours sitting here, thinking about it. I made up my mind to give you one more week. And then I was going to you. Come hell or high water, I was determined to get through to you.'' He gave a ragged laugh. "When you said my name, and I looked up and saw your lovely face, I wondered for a moment if I was dreaming.''

He stood up then, pulling her with him. Their arms went around each other, and they kissed and kissed as if they could never get enough.

"I love you," Max said at last, raggedly. "I love you so much, Samantha. You're part of me, darling, without you I don't have a life. I'll never let you leave me again.''

"I love you, too," she told him, her voice as ragged as his. "I never ever stopped loving you. I just wish I hadn't been so stubborn about Edna...I wish I'd let you explain. But I promise you, darling, I won't ever doubt you again.''

They kissed again. Passionate kisses, hungry kisses. Kisses that held the promise of lovemaking later, when they could be alone together in their bedroom.

"Annie," Max said suddenly. "Where's my Annie?''

"In the house with Helen. Let's go to her, Max.''

Hand in hand, they walked through the garden and up to the house. Annie must have seen them coming, because all at once there she was running to them.

"Daddy!" she shouted. "We're back!"

Max lifted her in his arms, and Samantha said, "We're back forever, Annie. We'll never leave again."

As Annie gave a shout of delight, the two adults smiled at each other.

"We are a family again," Max said. "Forever, my loves."

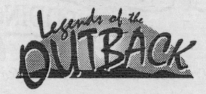

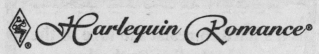

Harlequin Romance®

**On their very special day,
these brides and grooms are determined
the bride should wear white...
which means keeping passion in check!**

WHITE WEDDINGS

True love is worth waiting for...

Enjoy these brand-new stories from
your favorite authors

MATILDA'S WEDDING (HR #3601)
by **Betty Neels**
April 2000

THE FAITHFUL BRIDE
by **Rebecca Winters**
Coming in 2000

Available at your favorite retail outlet, only from

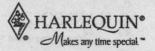

HARLEQUIN®
Makes any time special.™

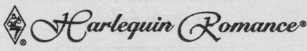

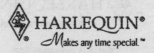